THE NEW DETECTIVE

Also by Peter Steiner

The Louis Morgon mysteries

LE CRIME
L'ASSASSIN
THE TERRORIST
THE RESISTANCE
THE CAPITALIST

The Willi Geismeier mysteries
THE GOOD COP *
THE CONSTANT MAN *
THE INCONVENIENT GERMAN *

* *available from Severn House*

THE NEW DETECTIVE

Peter Steiner

**SEVERN
HOUSE**

First world edition published in Great Britain and the USA in 2023
by Severn House, an imprint of Canongate Books Ltd,
14 High Street, Edinburgh EH1 1TE.

severnhouse.com

British Library Cataloguing-in-Publication Data
A CIP catalogue record for this title is available from the British Library.

ISBN-13: 978-1-4483-0642-8 (cased)
ISBN-13: 978-1-4483-0650-3 (e-book)

All Severn House titles are printed on acid-free paper.

MIX
Paper from
responsible sources
FSC   FSC® C013056
www.fsc.org

Typeset by Palimpsest Book Production Ltd.,
Falkirk, Stirlingshire, Scotland.
Printed and bound in Great Britain by
TJ Books, Padstow, Cornwall.

Praise for the Willi Geismeier mysteries

About the author

Peter Steiner is the author of the critically acclaimed Louis Morgon series of crime novels. He is also a cartoonist for *The New Yorker* and is the creator of one of the most famous cartoons of the technological age which prompted the adage, 'On the Internet, nobody knows you're a dog.'

MUNICH, NOVEMBER 1913

Sergeant Schobert looked his newest patrolman up and down. Willi Geismeier was nineteen. He looked like a schoolboy, tall, skinny, disheveled. But when Schobert looked him in the eye, there was something about how he looked back that made Schobert look away.

Willi's paperwork said he had graduated from the Royal Bavarian Police Academy at the top of his class – first in riding, first in marksmanship, first in everything. Schobert didn't like this new academy; he didn't see the need for it. In the old days you learned on the job. You just followed the tried-and-true ways and you'd be fine.

Someone being first in his class – he didn't like that either. And Willi was a rich kid. Plus, he had a sponsor in the upper police echelons, Chief Benno von Horvath. Schobert had heard about Horvath, one of those reformers – community policing, social justice, anti-corruption, that sort of thing.

He closed Willi's file. 'OK, Geismeier. I'm partnering you with Patrolman Heisse. He'll show you the ropes.'

Werner Heisse was old school in the worst sense. He had been a policeman for five years. He had tried for detective a few times, until he finally realized being a patrolman suited him better. As a patrolman with a regular beat, he could set things up to his advantage without anyone taking much notice. The protection he extorted from villains meant he always had money in his pocket. He just had to let the pimps and whores know who was boss from time to time, and he could have sex whenever it suited him. He got free drinks at the bars and clubs the same way. He'd just threaten to bring in a health inspector or to recommend that your license not be renewed. And he didn't have a wife or children to bother with. What more did he need?

Schobert warned Heisse about Willi. 'Don't worry,' said Heisse with a wink. His idea of showing Willi the ropes was to have him walk a night patrol alone through the toughest parts of the district. Schobert acted like he didn't know what Heisse meant. 'Whatever you think is best,' he said.

It was a poor neighborhood. The apartment blocks had been put up in a hurry in the late 1890s. Thanks to corruption in the building trades, they were already crumbling and should have been condemned. Few trees or shrubs could grow in the dark, narrow courtyards. The gas lights should have been on around the clock, but most of them had been destroyed. Drugs were sold and used freely in the courtyards. Prostitutes entertained their customers in hallways and abandoned rooms. Residents mostly cowered in their apartments.

Willi asked Heisse whether he would come along.

'Why? Are you scared, Geismeier?'

'A little,' said Willi. 'Besides, it's department policy that night patrols consist of two policemen,' said Willi.

'You know what's *my* department policy, Geismeier? That you damn well do what I tell you to do,' said Heisse.

Willi went alone. It was a warm night for November. He was new and in uniform, so when he approached a group of men standing about, they dispersed and sauntered off into the shadows. They leaned against a wall, hands in their pockets, and waited. But Willi didn't leave. Instead, he walked up to them.

'*Guten Abend*,' he said. 'What's going on?'

The men looked at each other. 'Nothing's going on, Herr *Wachtmeister*,' said one. 'We was just discussing the latest economic news.' The other men laughed.

'Really,' said Willi. 'And what do you think?'

The men looked at one another. 'What's your deal, copper?' said one. The others looked uncomfortable, ready for trouble.

'No deal,' said Willi. 'Just keeping the peace. Whatever you're doing, don't bother anyone and we'll be fine. I'll see you again soon. Have a good night.'

The men watched him go. 'What the devil was that?' said one.

'He's just a kid,' said another with a sneer. But he looked even younger than Willi.

A woman spilling out of a tiny dress stood by an alley waiting for customers. 'I'm meeting my husband,' she said when Willi came up. She dropped her cigarette on the pavement.

'I know,' said Willi.

'Where's Heisse?' she said.

'It's just me tonight,' said Willi. 'Willi Geismeier. Have a good night.'

Willi went into a bar. It was busy at this time of night, but it went quiet. 'Something to drink, officer?' said the bartender.

'A beer,' said Willi. Everyone was watching.

Willi reached into his pocket. 'On the house,' said the bartender.

'No thanks,' said Willi and laid a coin on the bar. The bartender stared at the coin for several seconds. Everyone else was looking at Willi, wondering what it meant that a policeman was paying for his own drink.

The next morning Willi found Werner Heisse in Schobert's office. 'How'd it go, Geismeier?' said Heisse. Willi took out his notebook and read from his notes: instances of drug dealing and prostitution.

'Did you bring them in?' said Schobert.

'No, I didn't,' said Willi.

'Why the hell not?' said Heisse. 'They were breaking the goddamn law. Did you let them feel your club, at least? Jesus!' Heisse was mad. He had hoped Willi would put his foot in it one way or the other and come back the worse for wear. Then he – Heisse – could go out there, reassure everyone and make everything right, remind the whores and dealers that as long as they kept up their side of the bargain, they had nothing to worry about. You had to remind them every once in a while what might happen if there was ever a straight cop on the beat.

'One drunk and disorderly,' said Willi, continuing his report. 'A Herr Metzger.'

'Metzger? *Herr* Metzger?' Heisse laughed. 'Did you at least bring *that* son of a bitch in?'

'I walked him home,' said Willi.

'You walked him home? Christ, Geismeier! We're not an escort service . . .'

'What Patrolman Heisse means, Geismeier, is that Walther Metzger is a real troublemaker. Sometimes it's drunk and disorderly, sometimes it's . . . he needs to be . . . kept in line. You know what I mean?'

'I think I do,' said Willi.

'Damn it, I knew that kid was gonna be trouble,' said Schobert as soon as Willi had left the office. He and Heisse spent the next hour trying to figure out how to get rid of Willi. The trouble was that Willi wasn't going to make it easy for them. As time went on, he walked the worst beats and took the worst shifts without complaining. He filed his paperwork on time. And he arrested thieves, bullies, muggers, even as he left the drug dealers and users, the whores and drunks alone.

Werner Heisse ordered a few of the dealers to beat Willi up. The next day Willi reported that he had been attacked by three men. He filed a detailed report on the event, including descriptions of the men Heisse had drafted to do the deed.

'I suppose now you're going to want medical leave?' said Schobert.

Willi said he was all right; no, he didn't need leave.

'You can't let them get away with that kind of behavior,' said Schobert.

'You should go back and beat the shit out of them,' said Heisse.

Later Schobert said to Heisse, 'Did you notice, Geismeier didn't seem to have a scratch on him?'

Heisse went back out and found the men. 'We gave him a good beating, Sergeant.' 'We made him pay, Sergeant, I swear.' They called Heisse Sergeant because they thought it flattered him.

'If I find out you're lying,' said Heisse, 'you'll regret it.' And then he punched one of them in the kidney just to let them know he meant business.

MURDER

Walther Metzger was found in the courtyard beaten to death. Willi and Heisse went out there together when the call came in. The neighborhood looked different in the daylight, still poor but less menacing. The dealers and whores were sleeping. A stooped old man with a stick was walking a dog that was even slower than he was. A woman pulled a small wooden cart with a bag of coal. A few people were standing back from Metzger's body watching the goings-on. One held a handkerchief over her mouth and nose, even though there was no smell.

The coroner was already there. 'Blunt force trauma,' he said when the two policemen walked up. 'Quite a few blows to the body and head with this.' He pointed to what looked like a table leg. There was hair and blood on it.

Heisse nudged the body with his foot and the coroner shot him a look. 'He was a useless piece of shit,' said Heisse. 'Come on, Geismeier. Let's go.'

'Where?' said Willi.

'Back to the station.'

'I'm going to look around,' said Willi.

'What for?' said Heisse.

'I'm going to look around,' said Willi again, and stooped down over the body beside the coroner.

Heisse looked at Willi. 'They'll be sending a detective, Geismeier. That's not your job.' Heisse waited for Willi to say something, but he didn't. Heisse figured, what the hell? If Willi wanted to get in the way of the detectives, fine with him. Heisse left, and Willi watched as the coroner went about his business.

'Was he drunk?' said Willi.

'He'd been drinking, but I don't know yet if he was drunk,' said the coroner.

'Anything in his pockets?' said Willi.

'A few coins,' said the coroner. 'One pocket was inside out, so maybe there was something else. But it's gone now.'

'Any sign of the table?' said Willi.

'The table?'

Willi pointed to the table leg.

'No,' said the coroner. 'Not my job.' He looked at Willi for the first time. 'You're new, aren't you?'

'Not that new,' said Willi.

'How long?'

'Two months.'

The coroner laughed then stood up with a sigh. 'Be careful,' he said.

'Careful?' said Willi. 'Of what?'

'Just be careful,' said the coroner. He nodded to the ambulance men.

They loaded Metzger's body into the ambulance and drove off, leaving Willi by himself. Most of the onlookers had drifted away, but Willi asked the three that remained whether they knew the victim. They all said they didn't.

Willi knocked on the door of the nearest apartment. It opened a crack. A security chain was in place. An old man looked out. Willi had seen him watching from the window. 'Did you know Walther Metzger?'

'Not really.'

'Do you know where he lived?'

'Upstairs. Two-B.'

'Were you friends?'

'No,' said the man.

'Had he lived there a long time?'

'I don't know.'

After a little prodding, Willi learned that the old man and Metzger had once been friends, but had fallen out.

'Why?' said Willi.

'Over a woman,' said the old man. 'It's true,' he said, seeing that Willi didn't believe him. 'But I didn't kill him.' The man's face dissolved and he let out a sob.

'Who was the woman?' Willi asked.

'Izabella,' said the old man. 'I don't know her last name.'

'Really?' said Willi. 'What *do* you know about her?'

'Just that she's called Izabella.'

'Who would have a key to Metzger's apartment?'

The old man closed the door and opened it again, leaving the chain in place, and reached out, handing Willi a key on a ribbon.

'Why do you have his key?'

'He would get sick sometimes. From drinking. I would help him out.'

'But you weren't friends?'

'No,' said the man.

'Do you have anything else of his?'

'No,' said the man.

'Thank you,' said Willi, holding up the key. 'I'll bring it right back.'

'Keep it. I don't need it any more,' said the man, and closed the door.

There was a sink across the hall from 2-B, and next to it was a rickety table. The leg that had been used to bludgeon Metzger had been torn from the table. Someone had stood the table back up on its three remaining legs. But there was debris on the floor – a broken bottle, a few dead flowers, a soap dish – that must have come from the table. The walls and floors were dingy, and there were flecks of blood on the wall.

Willi didn't need the key to get into the apartment; the door had been kicked in, splintering the molding and tearing the lock from the door. There was more blood inside the small kitchen. A door at the far end of the kitchen led into a bedroom. Each room had a window that looked out on the courtyard. The kitchen had a two-burner gas stove, a small ice box with butter, milk, eggs inside. There were a few jars and cans of food inside a built-in cupboard, along with a few pots, cups, saucers, bowls, plates. But it felt more like an office than a kitchen. A green table was pushed against the wall beside the window. There was a typewriter on it. There was a stack of various newspapers and books on the table as well. There were pencils, pens, an ink pot, a stack of blank paper, and two new ribbons in front of the typewriter. The table's drawer was empty. There were two chairs, one facing the desk and one beside it with more books on it, including some ledgers and law books. Some books were open, others had places marked with scraps of paper.

There were no pictures or personal mementos, except where someone had drawn a large raven directly on to the wall above the desk. The drawing was crudely done, in pencil, but with substantial detail. Whoever drew it couldn't draw well but knew ravens. If you were sitting at the desk, the raven was right in front of you.

The few notes in the margins of the books did not tell Willi anything. And other than these notes, there was nothing written or typed to be found. If Metzger had been working on something, it was gone.

The apartment was not in disarray, but it had been systematically searched. The typing paper, pencils, ribbons should have been in the table drawer and not on the table. The cans, jars, pans in the cupboard had all been crowded on to the bottom shelf while the other shelves were empty. The bedcovers had been pulled aside; clothes in the wardrobe had been pushed to the sides.

The wardrobe was over two meters tall. Willi brought a chair from the kitchen and climbed up on it. There was a clear spot in the dust on top of the wardrobe, from where something square, a box probably, had recently been removed. As he climbed down, Willi saw a button on the floor under the desk. It was brass, a uniform button. After examining the button, he put it back where he had found it.

Willi went down the hall to the toilet. He turned off the water and pulled the chain to flush the toilet. He stood on the seat to look into the water tank. People loved hiding stuff in toilet water tanks. But there was nothing there. He turned the water on again.

Willi knocked on the downstairs door again. 'What did Herr Metzger write? Do you know?'

The man shrugged and shook his head.

'Stories? Letters? What did he do for a living? Was he a writer or a lawyer or something like that?'

'He used to be a newspaper man,' said the man. 'Before he was a drunk.'

'Where?'

'Here.'

'For which paper?'

'The *Kurier*.'

'Was he still writing?' said Willi.

'Yes,' said the man. 'Every night.'

'How do you know?' said Willi.

The man pointed over his head. 'That typewriter clacked away all night. It kept me awake.'

The *Kurier* was one of the many small newspapers in Munich. It had offices on the fifth floor of an insurance office building in the city center. Willi asked to speak with someone who knew Walther Metzger. After a few minutes, a woman came out. She was pretty. She wore her glasses on top of her head, holding her bushy blonde hair in place. 'Izabella Bauer,' she said. They shook hands.

'Do you know Walther Metzger?' said Willi.

Yes, she said. Willi asked whether they could speak privately. She took him to a small conference room. He told her that Walther Metzger had been murdered and that he was investigating the murder. Her eyes got wide and then filled with tears. She sat down and covered her face with her hands while Willi waited.

Finally she looked up, her eyes red. 'How?'

'He was bludgeoned to death,' he said.

'Oh, God. Where did it happen?'

'At his home,' he said.

'I warned him,' she said, shaking her head.

Walther Metzger had spent fifteen years as an investigative reporter for the *Kurier*, mostly pursuing corruption – reporting how bribes were paid and lucrative contracts were improperly awarded for everything from office supplies to road repair. He had once written a series of stories exposing how contracts to lay streetcar tracks had been awarded to a criminal syndicate. Once the fraud was discovered, the new tracks were found to be improperly manufactured and had to be torn up and replaced. Half a dozen city employees went to prison, including a vice mayor and the procurement official in charge. But by then the principals in the syndicate had left for Argentina with suitcases filled with money. 'Walther was an excellent reporter,' said Izabella. 'Until he fell into the bottle.'

'Were you his editor?'

'Yes. I was an assistant editor at the time,' said Izabella. 'Then he got fired. I hadn't seen him for a long time. Then a few weeks ago he came to me with a story he had been working on. Corruption in the city government. I told him we couldn't use it. I said he should stop his investigation. It was too dangerous. He was a freelancer, on his own. He said he had to run this story down, to finish it one way or the other. This was his life, he said. Without journalism, he said, he might as well be dead.'

'Did he have any family?'

'No. He was alone. He wasn't married – never had been. No children.'

'Did you and Herr Metzger have a personal relationship?'

'We did once,' she said. 'But not now. Not for a long time.'

'Did you know his downstairs neighbor?'

'Detlev Schreier?' she said and smiled.

'He said he and Walther fell out over a woman named Izabella. Was that you?'

'Yes.' She smiled again. 'I think Detlev was in love with Walther too.'

Willi just looked at her for a moment while that sank in. 'What do you know about the story Walther was working on?' he said.

Izabella paused for a moment. 'How long have you been a policeman? You seem awfully young to be doing this.'

'I see,' said Willi, as though she had answered his question. 'So was he looking into the police department?'

'I don't know that. He just said it was corruption. That's all he told me.'

'That's pretty vague – corruption. You didn't ask him more about it? I mean, you warned him off the story, so you must have had some idea. You're a news editor. Weren't you even curious?'

'I didn't want to encourage him, so I didn't ask.'

'Frau Bauer, I am investigating Herr Metzger's murder. You know of course there are penalties for obstructing a police investigation. If you're withholding information that could help us find the people who killed Herr Metzger, that could be a crime in itself. What did he give you, either information or documentation about his investigation?'

'I'm sorry,' she said. 'I can't tell you any more.'

'Frau Bauer . . .' said Willi.

She stood up. 'I can't,' she said.

Willi saw that she was frightened. 'Have you been threatened?'

'I've told you everything I know,' she said.

'We'll see,' said Willi.

THE BOY DETECTIVE

One night after work, Willi went back to Walther Metzger's neighborhood. He asked the dealers and pimps what they knew. 'Ask Heisse,' said one.

There was nothing but dead ends. And Schobert piled on

the assignments, so Willi had to let it go. It wasn't his case, after all.

After another two months had passed and no one had been apprehended or charged with Walther Metzger's murder, Willi knocked on Sergeant Schobert's door.

'What is it, Geismeier?' said Schobert.

'I wonder, Sergeant, if you could tell me who's working on the Metzger case.'

'Who?' said Schobert.

'Yes. The name of the detective.'

'Why?' said Schobert.

'Well, nobody has been apprehended or charged, and I was wondering . . .'

'It's not your business to wonder, Geismeier. You want to be a detective, take the goddam detective exam. I'm sure you'll be at the top of the goddam class.' That police academy stuff still stuck in Schobert's craw. 'Just let me know if you don't have enough work, and I'll find you more. OK? Now get the hell out of here.'

Willi decided Schobert was right: he should become a detective. He studied after work, took the detective exam, and passed with flying colors, first in his class. He showed up at the precinct one day in plain clothes, knocked on Schobert's door and showed him the papers, officially making him a detective assigned to Schobert's squad. Schobert just stared at him.

'It was your suggestion, Sergeant. Remember?' said Willi. 'Thank you.'

Willi checked around and learned that the Metzger murder case had been closed. Someone upstairs had decided that it was better if whatever Metzger had been looking into never came to light.

The Metzger murder file and evidence box were buried in the police archives at the back of the Evidence Room, which is where Willi found them. The file was thin. There was the coroner's two-page report. There was a sketch of the crime scene with an outline of a body, the wounds marked and identified in pencil.

The report stated that Metzger had been attacked in the middle of the night. The body had been found early the next morning, when a man on his way to work nearly tripped over it. Metzger's door had been broken in and he had been bludgeoned with multiple blows from a table leg. Then he had been dragged down the stairs. He was probably dead by then.

The detective Richard Oberhof had knocked on doors up and down the hallway. A few of the neighbors – all named in the report – said they knew Metzger by sight, but none admitted to having heard or seen anything. Oberhof described the break-in but didn't mention the box missing from the top of the wardrobe. Maybe he just hadn't looked. He had interviewed Detlev Schreier and Izabella Bauer with unsatisfying results. But he didn't mention in his report anything about Walther Metzger investigating anything. He wrote only that he had discovered neither motives nor suspects in the case.

Oberhof didn't mention the peculiar scenario of the crime either. An extremely violent break-in and murderous assault followed by a thorough and remarkably unhurried search of the apartment. Wouldn't the perpetrator of such brutality have been desperate to get out of there as quickly as possible? The only way to understand the leisurely search of the apartment was that the assailant had no reason to fear the arrival of the police. He either knew the police wouldn't be coming or he was a policeman himself.

The evidence box was big. It had to be big to hold the bloody table leg. For some reason, Metzger's bloody jacket was in there too. Other than that, the box held only a logbook, a ledger, a bird identification book and a small pocket calendar.

The button wasn't there. And there was no record of it having been part of the evidence. Willi figured the button was missing for the same reason the case had been closed: the police believed the killer was one of their own.

The logbook, the ledger, and the bird book were labeled, 'From Victim's Kitchen.' The logbook and ledger appeared to be where someone had kept track of various transactions, official and unofficial. The bird book was well worn, and a number of the birds had dates and locations handwritten beside them.

The calendar was labeled, 'From Victim's Pocket.' At the scene, the coroner had said there was nothing in Metzger's pockets but a few coins. The calendar appeared to be Metzger's and had notations of meetings, identifying some people by initials, others by name. Willi found Izabella Bauer's initials on the day she said he had come to see her. He found an entry D.S. for Detlev Schreier on the day before he was murdered. Werner he identified by name now and then – 'Heisse,' perhaps on days when Werner had hit or arrested him. There was also an entry 'W.G.' on the day Willi had brought him home drunk. So Walther was a man who paid attention.

There were occasional notes, some medical – 'headache,' 'bloody urine,' 'diarrhea,' 'heart palpitations' – others more personal. He had noted Izabella's and Detlev's birthdays – only two weeks apart – and the birthdays of a few others. There were bird names and places here as well, probably indicating sightings – 'vireo, Nymphenburg.' And the dates matched most of those noted in the bird book. The calendar went back three years. Willi copied it all out; it took him most of a day to do it.

Willi went back to the scene again and talked to Metzger's neighbors one by one. He saw right away they were frightened of the police and wouldn't tell him anything. But one, Frau Blenheim, brought him into her apartment and gave him a cup of tea.

'How old are you?' she said.

Willi didn't answer.

She studied him and then shook her head. 'You're playing with fire, young man.'

'I'm investigating a murder,' said Willi.

'I know that,' she said. 'But that's not what the police do around here.'

'Did you hear anything that night?' said Willi.

'Of course I did. Everybody did. It was impossible not to hear it – the terrible screaming, the crashing . . .'

'But you didn't see anything,' said Willi.

'I made it a point not to. If you live here, you don't see or hear anything, if you know what's good for you.'

'Did you know Walther Metzger?' said Willi.

'A little,' she said. 'He seems . . . seemed nice.'

Willi talked to Izabella again. He told her about the box of papers taken from on top of the cupboard. He said he thought that was where Metzger had kept the work he was doing.

Izabella insisted again that Metzger hadn't told her what exactly he was investigating, only that it was big and dangerous and would send people to prison.

'Was Metzger ill?' said Willi.

'He was alcoholic,' said Izabella. 'Other than that, he seemed all right.'

'You don't know of any specific illness?'

'No.'

'Was he a birder?' said Willi.

'Yes, he loved birds. We took a birding trip down near Salzburg once. It was wonderful. Perfect weather and lots of birds. I loved him then.'

'Someone drew a pretty accurate raven on the wall above his desk. Would he have done that?'

'Yes, he might have. We once saw an albino raven. It was snow white with yellow eyes. A magnificent thing. It just sat there on a fence post and watched us. He thought of birds as messengers. He called them secret messengers from the gods.'

'Do you know what he meant?'

'Not exactly. He said they knew what we were up to. They flew back and forth between our world and the gods.' The recollection brought tears to her eyes.

Willi went back to Metzger's apartment. In the intervening months the apartment had been broken into repeatedly and was now being used as a shooting gallery. There were needles and bottles all over the place. Someone had tried to scratch out the drawing of the raven.

Heisse had talked about wanting to use a nightstick on Metzger. He would say that sort of thing often, mostly because he knew Willi was straight and it got his goat. Willi would get on his high horse about police corruption, like it was the world's greatest evil. If the police were corrupt there was nothing to hold Germany together, Willi said. The first time he said it, Heisse threatened to kick his ass, or have his boys do it for him. But that didn't stop Willi talking about police corruption. Eventually, Heisse would just stare at him like he was nuts.

At first Willi had thought that the police had killed Walther Metzger, even though he didn't think Heisse was involved. That brass button had gone missing because the police investigating the crime scene had found it and drawn the conclusion that someone among them was the killer. But what if that was the conclusion they were meant to draw? It was obvious that, after killing Metzger, the killer had searched the place carefully. He wouldn't have missed a shiny brass button lying in plain sight.

One day Willi and Heisse were in the office together. No one else was around. It was a slow afternoon. 'So, Werner,' said Willi, 'who do you think killed Metzger?'

Heisse swiveled in his chair and studied Willi for a moment. 'You're still snooping around that case, aren't you, Geismeier?'

'Maybe,' said Willi. 'So: what do you think happened?'

Heisse studied Willi again. 'Listen,' he said, 'you *know* what happened. Metzger stuck his nose in where he shouldn't have.'

'Yes, but where's that?' said Willi.'

Heisse laughed. 'You never let up, do you?'

'No,' said Willi. 'So where do you think he stuck his nose that got him killed? Do you think it's the police department?'

Heisse glared at Willi. But he didn't like the department higher-ups, so he considered the question. 'Well, he used to be a newspaper man. You know that, right? He specialized in scandals. So a lot of people – higher-ups – hated him and were afraid of his investigations. After all, he's brought down executives, politicians. Could have been anybody in that bunch.'

'Police?' said Willi.

Heisse ignored him.

'Trouble is, what they don't understand, Geismeier, the big shots, the jerks at the top, I mean: you get rid of one troublemaker like Metzger, there's always someone else ready to take his place. Killing Metzger, or the next guy, or the next, that doesn't solve your problem, does it? I mean Metzger's dead, but it all keeps going, doesn't it, the merry-go-round? The system works. A troublemaker's dead, the papers make a big deal out of it, the scammers scam, then the papers make a big deal out of *that*. They love crime and corruption, the papers; they can't get enough of it.

'Any one of those people that are always being investigated

– department heads, administrators, finance guys, police chiefs, you name it – could have wanted Metzger killed. Now he's dead. And what do they get by killing him?

'You and your corruption crap, Geismeier. It's the system, man. And the system works. Join the party or it will mow you down. So that's what I think. If I were you, Geismeier, I'd watch my ass.'

'Is that a warning?' said Willi.

Heisse gave Willi a sharp look. 'You're really asking for it, aren't you, Geismeier?'

'I guess so,' said Willi with a smile.

Heisse gave him a stare, then just had to laugh. He reached across the desk and gave Willi a little slap on the cheek. Willi thought it was friendly, but you never knew with Heisse.

28 JUNE 1914

'CORRUPTION!' was the headline in the morning's *Volkspresse*, the People's Press. *After a year-long investigation, a team of reporters at the* Volkspresse *has uncovered a pattern of corruption in the highest ranks of the Munich city government. The corruption reaches across multiple departments, including transportation, police, parks and forests, and public health. The corruption is widespread and involves multiple current and past officials.* It came two weeks after Willi and Werner Heisse had had their little talk, and it was just like Werner had said.

Willi realized he had been thinking too narrowly about the case. There was the corruption, of course, but that was not the whole story or even the main story. Walther Metzger's life, like everyone's, was more complicated than what he was working on. Willi started going through Munich's newspapers, going back six months and studying the corruption stories. Every week or two there was another one; you could depend on it. With each story he found he tried, with no luck, to match the initials and dates from Walther's calendar with names in the stories. But now with the *Volkspresse* story there were some matches: initials and dates.

Willi called Izabella Bauer and asked to see her. She didn't seem surprised to hear from him.

But when he got there the next morning, she said, 'I'm sorry, I don't have time.' Before he could press her, she handed him a cablegram. 'This just came in: somebody shot and killed Franz Ferdinand and his wife.'

'When?' said Willi.

'Just now,' she said.

Willi read the cablegram. 'Sarajevo. This means war, doesn't it?' said Willi.

'War,' said Izabella. 'Probably. Yes.'

It had been a long time coming. Willi turned and looked out the window at the leaden sky above the buildings across the street. The first drops of rain began splashing against the windows, like a harbinger of something awful.

Izabella looked at Willi. A young man like him was going to be drafted as soon as the fighting started. Willi and Izabella stood there, lost in their own thoughts, trying to grasp what had changed for them, what the future held for them, for everyone.

You had to go on with life as it was, not as you imagined it was about to become. 'I have a few questions,' Willi said. 'Did you see the corruption story in the *Volkspresse*?'

'Oh, yes,' said Izabella and laid the cable aside. 'I guessed that's what you wanted to talk about.'

'Have you read the story?'

'Yes, but not closely; this . . .' She waved her hand, as though Sarajevo were right outside the window. It was raining hard now.

'What's your first reaction to the story? Is this the kind of thing Walther Metzger might have somehow been involved in?'

'It might be, but I really don't know.'

'Were you surprised to see the *Volkspresse* story?'

'No, not really. We've been working on civil corruption too. This is Munich, after all.'

'So it's not unusual for different papers to be working on the same thing at the same time?' said Willi.

'Not at all,' said Izabella. 'It would be unusual if we *weren't*.

We have the same sources, and a corruption story sells papers. Every editor is pushing his reporters in that direction. And the reporters are competing to get the story first. As I said, corruption is always a story in Munich, and we always have someone working on it.'

'Do you know any of the *Volkspresse* people in the byline?'

'I'm sorry, Sarajevo . . . is this really that urgent?'

'It's murder and corruption,' said Willi. 'What do you think?'

She sighed, then looked at the paper. 'Three of them,' she said.

Willi wrote down their names.

'And what about *your* people on the corruption beat? Could I talk to them?'

She gave him the names.

Ruprecht Brecht was at his desk looking through financial ledgers when Willi came up. 'Herr Brecht, can I talk to you for a minute?' said Willi.

'I'm busy,' said Ruprecht without looking up.

'I'm a police detective,' said Willi. 'Geismeier.'

Now Ruprecht looked up. Then he snorted. 'What do you want?'

'I'm investigating a murder . . .' said Willi.

Brecht snorted again. 'Whose?' he said.

'. . . and corruption,' said Willi.

Now Ruprecht laughed outright. 'A cop interested in corruption? Don't make me laugh.'

'You already laughed,' said Willi. 'Maybe you can tell me what's funny. So I can laugh too.'

A smile flickered across Ruprecht's face, but he gave Willi a considering look and decided not to say anything clever about boy detectives. He placed a sheet of paper to mark his place and closed the ledger. 'Pull up that chair, Detective . . .'

'Geismeier,' said Willi again, and pulled the chair over beside Ruprecht's desk. He sat down and took a small notebook from his jacket pocket.

'Fire away,' said Ruprecht.

'How do you know when you've got corruption?' said Willi.

Ruprecht stared at Willi. 'What kind of question is that?'

'A fairly easy one, I would think. Do you start with the assumption that everything and everyone is corrupt? What's the first thing that tells you there's corruption going on? Does it start with a hunch, a clue, a tip?'

'Rarely a hunch, sometimes a tip, usually a clue,' said Ruprecht.

'And how do you recognize that it's corruption?'

'Something smells, Detective. Something doesn't feel right, doesn't add up. Isn't it the same for you?'

'How did the *Volkspresse* get the story before you did?'

'They got ahead of themselves, that's how,' he said. 'Their story won't stick. Half the people they've arrested are gonna walk. They don't have the witnesses; they don't have the documentation. Let me show you something.'

Ruprecht opened the ledger. It was from the Munich Hospital administration. Over the next fifteen minutes, Ruprecht explained how money had been dispensed for medical supplies and services, but the supplies could not be located and the services had never been dispensed. There were discrepancies in the ledger, but they had been papered over by receipts which now appeared to be fake. And the signatures authorizing the purchases and on the receipts were not real, and there was no evidence as to who had written or signed those documents. 'So the guy they mention in the *Volkspresse* – a Doctor Vietor – is already suing the paper for defamation. He may be the guy, but they haven't proved it. They made the same mistakes with other departments – including the police.'

'Tell me,' said Willi.

'They've got an assistant police chief protecting the guy that owns his gambling debts. But all they've got is the word of the bookie. Hey, I thought you said you were looking into a murder.'

'I am,' said Willi. 'Do you know the guys that wrote the *Volkspresse* piece?'

'Some of them,' said Ruprecht.

'Are any of them any good?'

'Some of them.'

'What about the lead guy, Arenz?'

'You're the detective,' said Ruprecht. 'Find out for yourself.'

HELMUTT ARENZ

Helmutt Arenz was the lead reporter on the *Volkspresse* corruption story. Willi went back to Izabella. 'Tell me about Helmutt Arenz,' he said. 'Do you know him personally?'

'Yes,' said Izabella. 'He used to work here.'

'As a reporter?'

'Yes.'

'When was that?' said Willi.

'About eight or ten years ago. I'd have to check to be sure.'

'And was Walther Metzger working here at the same time?'

'I think they overlapped for a few months.'

'And you can remember they overlapped for a few months, even though it might have been ten years ago?'

'I remember because they were sort of friends.'

'So they knew each other pretty well?'

'Yes.'

'Did they remain in touch?'

'I don't know,' said Izabella.

'Why did Arenz leave the paper?'

'The *Volkspresse* offered him more money.'

'Were you sorry to lose him?'

'No, not really. He was unreliable. He cut corners.'

'What do you mean?'

'He didn't do the work – the research, the legwork – the stuff you have to do to get a story.'

'So, were you surprised when you saw that Arenz had written this particular story?'

'No, I still haven't read the whole story. But maybe he's finally pulled himself together. If so, I'm glad to hear it.'

'Do you think Walther could have been working with Helmutt Arenz?'

'No. Definitely not. Walther was a loner.'

'You said Walther was a good reporter?'

'Walther was the best.'

Helmutt Arenz was waiting for Willi at his desk at the *Volkspresse*. Willi had called to say he wanted to talk.

'About what?' said Helmutt.

'About Walther Metzger. I'm looking into his murder.'

'Yeah, I heard about that. Poor guy,' said Helmutt. 'Terrible business.'

When Willi showed up, Helmutt was at his desk, feet up, puffing on a cigar. Some of his coworkers were hanging around, laughing and bantering. Helmutt shooed them away, and motioned for Willi to sit down. He opened a box of Havana cigars and held it toward Willi. 'Have one,' he said. 'I'm celebrating my big story.'

'Congratulations,' said Willi.

'First in a series,' he said. 'It's going to blow the lid off things.'

'It is quite a story, Herr Arenz. You must be proud,' said Willi. 'I look forward to the next installment.' But he didn't take a cigar. 'So, I just have a few questions regarding Walther Metzger, if you don't mind.'

'Not at all,' said Helmutt.

'How well did you know him?'

'Not very well,' said Helmutt, and put out his cigar in the ashtray. 'We were at the *Kurier* at the same time, but I didn't know him except to say hello. I hadn't seen him for a long time. He started drinking heavily, you know, and he stopped working, as far as I know. Last time I saw him, he was unfriendly – the alcohol, I think. Hostile. I think he was jealous, that I had this job and was breaking stories, and he wasn't. I don't know; it was sad.'

'Would you be surprised to know that he was working right up to the end?'

'Really? Who for?'

'I heard he was working on a corruption story of his own?'

'Really? No, I didn't know that.'

'So you wouldn't have any idea whether you and he were covering the same ground?'

'No idea. It's possible, but it seems unlikely.'

'Why unlikely?' said Willi.

'Well, none of my sources ever indicated to me that they had talked to anyone besides me. Not a single one. So he must have been working on something else, if he was working on anything at all.'

'You don't believe he was?'

'Well, I don't know, of course. But the last I heard he was drunk most of the time.'

'Did you read any of the stories about his murder?'

'A few. I've followed it a little,' said Helmutt. 'I knew the guy. The police are a little "stuck," aren't they?'

'Well, my thinking is Metzger was looking into corruption in the police department,' said Willi.

'Well, that would be fertile ground, wouldn't it, Detective?' Helmutt grinned. 'That's probably what got him killed.'

'So you think the police had him killed?' said Willi.

'I don't know, Detective. That's your line of work. I'm just guessing, but it seems pretty likely, doesn't it?'

'Likely?' said Willi.

'Well, they found evidence, didn't they?'

'You mean the button?' said Willi.

'Yeah, the button,' said Helmutt. 'From a police uniform, wasn't it?'

'Yes, it was,' said Willi. He paused to write something in his notebook. 'Herr Arenz, you mentioned your sources. Do you think I could talk to some of them, just to find out whether Walther had been in touch with them? They might have useful information.'

Helmutt laughed. 'You know, Detective, a reporter can't reveal his sources. It'd be unethical. And, besides, no one would ever talk to me again, would they?'

'So you had people inside the government that talked to you?'

Helmutt smiled. 'I'm not saying who talked to me, Herr Detective.'

'How long have you been working on this story?' said Willi.

'Three years.'

'That's impressive,' said Willi.

'This business is all about patience and legwork,' said Helmutt.

'Following leads wherever they take you. A little like your work, isn't it, Herr Detective?'

'Maybe,' said Willi. 'Except I have to get it right.'

'What do you mean?' said Helmutt.

'Well,' said Willi. 'You don't, do you? Everybody knows half of what's in the paper is made up.'

'What are you saying?' said Helmutt.

'Lawsuits are already being filed against you and the *Volkspresse*. I've heard that you cut corners.'

Helmutt stood up, his fists clenched. He took a step toward Willi.

'Take it easy, Helmutt,' said the man at the next desk. He came over and stepped between the two men. 'He was just joking. Weren't you, Detective?'

'No,' said Willi. 'No, I wasn't.'

The exposé in the *Volkspresse* laid out in broad outlines a web of corruption that, the article said, went across various departments in both the city government and the Bavarian government. It named some of the culpable who had already been indicted, others who had resigned, and some who had made a run for it and were no longer around to be questioned. The article was sketchy and short on specifics.

Not surprisingly, nearly everyone named had either referred the reporter to his attorney without comment or proclaimed his innocence. Willi decided nothing useful could be gained by talking to them. Toward the end of the article, though, he read about Graf (Count) Sigismund Maria von Wittelsbach, a second cousin of Ludwig the Third, the king of Bavaria.

The count, who owned a large estate in the Bavarian Forest and lived in a palace in Munich, had been caught up in the scandal, much to his chagrin. Years earlier, having been injured in a riding accident, the count had landed in a municipal hospital. And while his treatment was swift and excellent, he had been appalled to see how the lower classes were treated or, more accurately, were mistreated. Even the seriously ill and grievously injured waited in wretched conditions to get the most perfunctory care. When he inquired about this, he was told there was nothing to be done; all public health and all treatment protocols were regulated by Munich's public health commissioners.

The count served on a number of boards and commissions already, and now he had himself appointed to Munich's public health commission hoping to improve public health for his fellow citizens. According to the *Volkspresse*, Munich's public health commission had been granting licenses to corrupt hospital administrators for years. Some administrators, yet to be named, had been receiving bribes and kickbacks from favored providers of hospital services – ambulance companies, hospital suppliers, even doctors. They had also been collecting consulting fees and skimming money from public hospital budgets.

Although the count had been shown to know nothing about any of this, he felt culpable nonetheless. 'I should have made it my business to know,' he said. 'It is my duty as a Wittelsbach to accept responsibility for criminal behavior on my watch. Of course I will endeavor to make things whole.'

Noblesse oblige, thought Willi; *here is a witness who might tell the truth.*

GRAF SIGISMUND MARIA VON WITTELSBACH

Willi sat on a gilt chair in an anteroom between two tapestries depicting a stag hunt. In one the stag was leaping through the forest with wild eyes; in the other he was down, his tongue out, his eyes wild with fear, as dogs tore at his flesh.

Willi had written to the count asking for an interview, explaining that he was a police detective investigating a crime that might be connected somehow to the fraud in the Munich public health commission. The count wrote back, agreeing to answer his questions to the best of his ability, either in writing or in person. Willi wrote back saying he favored a personal interview.

After a few minutes, the count's secretary came out and walked Willi down a hallway to a wood-paneled office, decorated with the mounted heads of stags and chamois, racks of guns, riding and racing trophies, and paintings of the count's favorite horses and dogs. Count Sigismund rose from his desk and offered Willi his hand. He was elderly and, to Willi's surprise, was wearing the uniform of a cavalry officer. He had thinning white hair, mutton chops and a mustache. A *pince-nez* hung on a thin gold chain from the top button of his tunic. A plumed helmet and a sword lay on a table by the window.

'Have you been called up too, Herr Graf?' said Willi.

'I am rejoining the Second Austrian Ulans, Herr Geismeier. I served with them when I was young. And you, I assume, will have received orders as well?'

'Yes, Herr Graf, I report on the first of July. Also the Ulans.'

'Two weeks then. Do you ride?'

'Yes, Herr Graf. Do you think there will be much riding in this war?'

'There's always riding in a war, Herr Geismeier. Nobody can maneuver like the cavalry. Well, neither of us has much time then, do we?' He gestured toward a chair and sat down across from him. 'It is Detective Geismeier?' he said.

'Yes,' said Willi. 'Detective.'

The count nodded. 'Detective Geismeier then, how can I help you?'

'Herr Graf, you are quoted in the article in the *Volkspresse* as saying' – Willi referred to his notebook – '"even though I didn't know about the theft, I should have." I wonder: *could* you have known? Did you have some sense that there was criminal activity, that something was wrong?'

'Detective Geismeier, as you might imagine, I have given this question a lot of thought over the last several weeks. I didn't have any sense that anything was wrong in the commission. But in retrospect, I am amazed at the depth of my ignorance. Many of the commissioners were congenial men, but some of them were businessmen with interests in medical supplies and pharmaceuticals and real estate, interests that were sometimes in conflict with their duty as commissioners to improve Munich's public health-care system. Others were physicians, but with business interests that might have been in conflict with their medical responsibilities. Some of these men seem now to have been untrustworthy on the face of it, although I don't know whether they seemed honest because of their manners or because of . . . how shall I say it? . . . because of the prejudices of my class.

'Also, there were meetings going on between certain members of the commission, meetings I was not privy to, meetings where decisions were being made and actions were being taken. I did not inquire about these actions, and I should have. I absolutely should have.'

'And is it your sense, Herr Graf, that the bribery within the public health commission was connected to criminal activity in other government departments?'

'I have no doubt that is the case,' said the count.

'There was nothing about that in Herr Arenz's article. Was that not something he asked you about?'

'No, he didn't. When Herr Arenz interviewed me, he had already collected most of the facts in the case, so he had very few questions. He mostly wanted me to confirm information he already had.'

'Did that surprise you, Herr Graf?'

'Not really. Why should it? He was being careful. He was merely confirming what I and others had already told his colleagues.'

'His colleagues? You mean he was not the first reporter you spoke with?'

'No. I had already been thoroughly interviewed by another reporter. He had come to me with a great many questions, which I answered as best I could. In fact, I'm embarrassed to say, he's the one who informed me about the goings-on in the public health commission.'

'When was this?' said Willi.

'Oh, maybe three months ago. I told the other reporter what I knew, and he put what I knew together with what he already knew. We met several times.'

'Three months ago?'

'Maybe four,' said the count. 'I confess, I was surprised when Herr Arenz showed up. I had pretty much given up on the story ever coming out, it had been so long since I had been interviewed that first time.'

'Do you remember the name of Arenz's colleague, the person who interviewed you those months ago?'

'I knew you were going to ask me that,' said the count. 'My secretary could probably find it in my appointment book.'

'Could it be Walther Metzger?' said Willi.

'I don't know,' said the count. 'My memory.' He passed his hand across in front of his face. 'I remember he was a somewhat abrasive man, poorly dressed, and smelling of alcohol.'

Willi checked Metzger's calendar and found the count's initials five months earlier. Two days later, Willi received a note from the count's secretary confirming that Walther Metzger had interviewed the count on three separate occasions, twice in January and once in February.

THE GREEN-EYED MONSTER

Willi went back to Izabella once more to ask whether Walther had said anything about documents or other evidence he was collecting.

'He only said he had proof of everything,' she said, 'but he didn't tell me what that everything was.'

'Would he have hidden his proof somewhere, or would he have had it at home?'

'He would have needed it with him,' said Izabella, 'and he was working at home. Why are you asking?'

'What might he have done to safeguard this material?' said Willi.

'From whom?' said Izabella.

'From anyone,' said Willi. 'He was investigating lots of very important people.'

'I don't know what he could have done. It's risky for any reporter investigating corruption to have papers – notes, documents – around,' said Izabella. 'But at the same time he needs to refer to them. And Walther always had to check and double-check everything. Nobody can keep that kind of material in his head, certainly not Walther. So it was a risk he would have had to take.'

Walther Metzger had not been killed by the police or anyone else he had been investigating. Helmutt Arenz – jealous of Metzger's acumen as a journalist and desperate to make a career for himself – had killed him in a fit of jealous fury. That he knew about the button had given him away. Willi was also certain that the box missing from the top of Walther's wardrobe held notes and records about the crimes he was investigating.

Maybe Arenz had visited Walther. Maybe he had tried to persuade Walther to let him in on the story. They had been friends, after all. There was enough for them both. But Metzger refused and Helmutt left angry. Then he thought: Metzger was just a useless drunk. His investigation would never see the light of day. And Helmutt could make good use of what Metzger had found. He would put together the story, publish it, and finally have the successful career that had so far eluded him.

The next day Helmutt went back. Walther wasn't there so he broke in. Walther came home while his place was being ransacked, and Helmutt went into a rage and beat him to death. But the papers were nowhere to be found. He left the button to cover his tracks.

Willi knocked on Detlev Schreier's door. Schreier didn't respond.

'I know you're in there, Herr Schreier. Open the door.'

'Go away,' said Schreier. 'Leave me alone.'

'I'm not going away, Herr Schreier, until you answer some questions. You can answer my questions now, or you can deal with the killer when he comes back to shut you up.'

Schreier opened the door with the safety chain in place. 'What do you want? I told you everything I know. I didn't see or hear anything.'

'Herr Schreier, if Walther's typing kept you from sleeping, then you heard him being killed. It was loud and it was brutal. He was slammed against the wall over and over. He was struck over and over with a club, his head was caved in, he would have screamed . . .'

'Stop!' shouted Schreier. 'Just stop!' Schreier put his hands over his ears as though he were hearing the assault all over again. He opened the latch and let Willi in, then closed the latch with trembling hands. Willi went to the sink and got him a glass of water.

'You saw whoever did it, and they threatened you. They said you'd better keep quiet or you'd get what Walther got.'

'I didn't see them,' Schreier said, 'I swear.' He was whimpering.

'Them?' said Willi.

'Him,' said Schreier. 'I didn't see anyone.'

'What about a box? Did they have a box when they threatened you? Were they carrying a box about this big?'

'I don't have it,' said Schreier.

'What do you mean you don't have it? *Did* you have it? Are you saying you had it at one time?'

'No. Yes. I don't know.' He drank some more water. 'Walther gave me a box to keep for him.'

'When was this?'

'The night before he was killed. Walther said there were people who wanted it.'

'Did he say what was inside?'

'No. But I looked inside. It was notebooks, papers, documents, stuff like that.'

'Will you show me?' said Willi.

'I can't.'

'Herr Schreier . . .'

'I don't have it any more.'

'Where is it?' said Willi.

'He took it.'

'Who took it?'

'He saw me looking out. He said he knew I had it. I don't know how he knew. He said I'd better give it to him or he would kill me. He said if I told anyone he would . . . I would get what Walther got.' Schreier broke down sobbing.

When Willi came back with a photo of Helmutt Arenz, Schreier said that was the man and started sobbing all over again.

Policemen were reporting to work in military uniforms these days, and then leaving for the front. Both Schobert and Heisse had been called up and, like Willi, were due to leave any day.

The police department would soon be made up of those deemed unfit for combat for one reason or another. That didn't mean they were bad policemen, they were told. Just that they would have to leave the fighting to others.

Heisse said he was looking forward to the war. 'We'll win it quick,' he said. 'It'll be a change. Better than all this shit.' He had grown bored with his own corruption.

'Let's go have a beer,' said Willi.

'What do you want, Geismeier?'

'Is that a yes?' said Willi.

'Are you buying?' said Heisse.

It was a hot afternoon. There was no breeze. They sat across from one another at one of the long tables in the cool basement of the Hofbräuhaus. They sipped their beer in silence for a while.

'I found Walther Metzger's killer,' said Willi.

Heisse peered at Willi across the top of his glass and set it back down. 'What do you mean?' said Heisse. Then: 'Are you crazy?'

'Metzger had the goods on all sorts of corrupt big shots,' said Willi.

'And now you're going to tell me it's a cop that killed him. You know, don't you, that all you're doing is putting a bull's-eye on your own back?'

'You're wrong,' said Willi.

'Just leave me out of it,' said Heisse. 'You crazy son of a bitch,' he added for good measure.

'It's not what you think,' said Willi. He told Heisse the story.

'Jesus Christ,' said Heisse. Then he laughed. 'And now you're stuck with this information, Geismeier. Am I right? You were ordered off the case, so if you tell anyone, your ass is in a sling. Am I right?'

'Do you know a detective named Richard Oberhof?' said Willi.

'Yeah, I know him,' said Heisse.

'He was the guy they assigned to the case,' said Willi.

'Yeah, I know,' said Heisse. 'So that he could shut it down. Which he did.'

'Well, don't you think he might be interested in reopening it now? I mean, think about it: the guy writing in the newspaper about all the corruption turns out to be a killer. So if Oberhof can find those missing files and arrest him, then the investigation and the evidence all goes away.'

Detective Oberhof didn't want anything to do with it. After all, he had found the button and then tucked it away only he knew where. He had suppressed evidence and obstructed justice, itself a serious criminal offense. Willi persuaded him that making the case would not depend on the button as evidence.

Detective Oberhof was convinced that arresting Arenz would be a big feather in his cap, and it would also be good for the department. All they had to do to make the case stick was find the missing files in Arenz's possession. Oberhof explained all this to his captain and then to the precinct chief. 'So, you don't have the files,' said the chief.

'Not yet,' said Detective Oberhof, 'but I will shortly.'

'Do you know where they are?' said the captain.

'Arenz is writing on deadline, so he needs to have those files handy. They're in the building somewhere.'

'And, assuming you find the files . . .'

'Oh, we'll find them,' said Oberhof.

'Well, assuming you find them, what will become of them?' said the captain.

'Once we have them,' said Oberhof, 'they become evidence in a murder investigation. They go into the Evidence Room and nobody will ever see them again. Ever. Of course, information in them can be used to advance police investigations, solve cases. But that's all.'

'And at our discretion,' said the chief.

'Of course,' said Oberhof. 'Yes. At your discretion. That goes without saying.'

Helmutt Arenz was typing away when Oberhof and Heisse showed up at his desk. When they said they were from the police, he closed the little notebook beside the typewriter and asked what they wanted. Oberhof picked up the notebook. Helmutt reached for it, and Heisse slammed him back in his chair.

'Are these your notes?' said Oberhof.

'Yes, of course,' said Arenz, 'and you don't have any right to take them.' He was trying to sound indignant, but the conviction had already gone out of his voice. 'What's this all about?'

Oberhof told him to pick up a pencil and write '12 January 1913. Vice mayor confirmed meeting.'

Arenz refused until Heisse grabbed a pencil and stuffed it into his clenched fist. Despite his best effort, his handwriting didn't look anything like the writing in the notebook. After a brief search, a team of policemen turned up the box of papers in a storage locker in the basement of the building. One of the cleaners told them that Helmutt came to the locker regularly. 'I thought it was to sneak a drink,' he said.

Helmutt Arenz was arrested. Walther Metzger's papers were taken to a shelf deep in the departmental Evidence Room, just as Detective Oberhof had speculated they would be. Half of official Munich breathed a sigh of relief. That same afternoon, Detective Willi Geismeier signed into the Evidence Room, which was his right as a detective in the Munich police department, and spent the rest of the day going through the Metzger files.

Ten days later, on the day Detective Richard Oberhof and Patrolman Werner Heisse were being awarded departmental commendations, Willi Geismeier, in uniform, carrying a rucksack and a rifle, sitting on a crowded wooden bench in a third-class railroad car with hundreds of other German men, was on his way to Belgium and the war. Coincidentally Graf Sigismund Maria von Wittelsbach was in a first-class carriage in the rear of the same train. And his horse Abendstern was in the adjoining car with all the other officers' horses.

8 NOVEMBER 1917

The hospital – in what had been a country school – was filled with sick and wounded men. Every day ambulances came up the gravel drive and newly injured men were rushed in on stretchers, or limped in supported by medics.

The intake room had once been the headmaster's office. Now it contained rows of cots full of moaning and crying men. The triage officer, wearing a heavy mask against the stench, sent those who could be saved to the makeshift surgery. Those who were done for were given morphine, which quieted them down. Then they were taken elsewhere to die.

The front was only three kilometers to the north. When the shelling got heavy, the windows rattled in sympathy. The sky was often filled with smoke that the sun turned a sickening shade of orange. It was like a noisy, endless opera of suffering and death.

In the main ward where the survivors tried to recover, the nurses and doctors hurried from bed to bed on their rounds. Drawings by long-gone schoolchildren still hung on the walls – there was a square house with yellow smoke curling from a blue chimney, a family of six stick figures hand in hand, a red dog and a green cat.

'Sergeant Geismeier?' said the doctor.

'Yes, sir,' said Willi.

The doctor studied the chart, then peeled off the bandages that had been covering Willi's eyes. 'Ypres?' he said. Ypres had been the scene of multiple gas attacks on both sides. It was where chemical warfare was born.

'Yes, sir,' said Willi.

'The damned British!' said the doctor.

'This time it was us,' said Willi. 'Our own gas blew back on us. We can't control the wind, you know.'

'This time?' said the doctor.

'I was gassed back in '15.'

'It says you were in intelligence,' said the doctor. Willi could hear him busying himself with his chart.

'Yes,' said Willi.

Finally the doctor said, 'You've been in hospital how long, Geismeier?'

It was on the chart, but Willi answered anyway. 'Two weeks this time.'

'Open your eyes, Sergeant,' said the doctor. 'What do you see?'

'Nothing,' said Willi.

The doctor swung his hand by Willi's face, just to check that he wasn't malingering.

'Nothing,' said Willi again, feeling the breeze.

'No shapes, no colors?' said the doctor.

'Is gray a color?' said Willi.

'Gray. So. Good. Is it brighter than it was with the bandages on?'

'Not really,' said Willi.

He looked at the scars on Willi's arm and shoulder.

'That's all healed nicely,' he said. 'Do you have any pain?'

'Not much,' said Willi. 'That's all from earlier.'

'Good,' said the doctor. Willi wondered what was good about it.

'Are the bandages off my eyes for good?' said Willi.

'I think so,' said the nurse. The doctor had moved on. 'Can I get you something to eat or drink?' She had a sweet voice, soft, a little husky, not young. A northern accent, Hamburg maybe, or Lübeck.

'Some water, thanks,' said Willi.

He sniffed before he drank, like it was a glass of wine. Even after two weeks, he was surprised when the water didn't smell or taste of sulfur.

The nurse read down his chart. 'Well, would you look at that. It's your birthday!'

'Yes,' said Willi.

'Friday the eighth. Let's see, that makes you . . .' Willi let her work it out. 'Twenty-three.'

She took Willi's hand and squeezed it. 'My Klaus is twenty-two.'

'Is he?' said Willi.

'He's in Belgium too. I think. Somewhere.'

'I hope he's all right,' said Willi.

'Yes,' she said. 'Thank you. I hope so.' She held his hand for a few seconds more, then moved on to the next cot.

After a few days without his eyes bandaged, Willi could make out the nurses and doctors as dark shapes. Every day he was visited by a different doctor. They all smelled like disinfectant and wore protective masks. Today's doctor leaned over and lifted Willi's eyelids. He shined a light into first one eye, then the other. He moved the light around and told Willi to follow it with his eyes. He held up four fingers and asked Willi how many he saw.

'Four,' said Willi.

'Excellent,' said the doctor.

Willi could find his way around the ward now. He could make out the rows of cots and the shapes of men lying on them. The windows still blinded him. He carried the white stick they had given him. He had to put his face very close to the wall to see the children's drawings.

He wasn't supposed to go outside, but he did anyway, just to breathe the cold air, to feel it on his face and hands, to be able to stand up without being shot at, to be away from the moaning and snoring and coughing. Still the artillery thumping in the distance reminded him where he was and where he had been. Sometimes he would cover his ears, but it didn't do any good.

When the doctor held up the eye chart, Willi could make out the largest letters. And his eyes had stopped watering. Still, when he tried to read a sonnet from his Shakespeare, all he saw were fourteen fuzzy gray lines of type across the page. He had trouble seeing anything in bright light. He couldn't see faces clearly, and colors were dull.

He was fitted with thick glasses. With the glasses he could see better. If he held the book close to his face, he could make out words 'the darling buds of May,' but it still wasn't exactly reading. Most of the time he didn't need the white cane. Just on uneven ground or at night going through the ward to the latrine.

'It will continue to improve,' said a doctor one day. 'We're sending you home. Good luck, Sergeant.' Just like that.

Willi put on his uniform, put his kit together, and reported to the hospital director to be officially discharged.

'I know you're disappointed, Sergeant,' said the colonel as he signed Willi's papers. Willi stood at attention.

'I know you'd like to get back to your comrades.' He paused.

Willi was supposed to say 'Yes, sir!' but he didn't say anything.

'Germany hasn't won the war yet, Sergeant. But thanks to you and millions of other brave young men like you, we're well on the way.'

Willi knew that was a lie. They were sending schoolboys and old men to the front now. And America had just come into the war.

'You've done your part, Sergeant,' said the colonel. *'This* proves it.' He pointed to the medals pinned on Willi's chest and then tapped them, in case Willi couldn't see him pointing. 'His Majesty, the Kaiser, thanks you.'

Willi saluted the colonel, did an about-face, and left the war.

MUNICH AGAIN

The train ride home took three days. The train would stop unexpectedly, sometimes to make way for a train taking soldiers to the front, and sometimes for no apparent reason. Sometimes it was the middle of the night, and the passengers, mostly soldiers, including the wounded, would be ordered off the train. They would crowd into the station as best they could. It would be warm, at least, and if you were lucky, there was turnip soup and black bread. But sometimes there was only a platform and they waited outside in the cold. Or they just sat in a car on a siding in the cold and the dark.

The cars were crowded and they stank. There were not enough seats for everyone. Willi had to stand after they left Frankfurt. His white cane didn't count for anything. Lots of men were worse off than that.

A few men talked or played cards. But mostly you heard coughing or snoring or moaning, pretty much the same as in the hospital. In Stuttgart they took a guy off the train who had died where he sat. Nobody had realized he was dead until they had all stood up to get off. 'Hey, *Kamerad*!' somebody said, and nudged his shoulder. He fell over. The entire back of his shirt was soaked in blood. They all filed past the dead guy to get off the train. To die on your way home . . .

The last leg of Willi's trip – the train from Stuttgart to Munich – had more civilians than soldiers on it. Willi sat down facing a middle-aged couple with a young girl. Her grandparents, he thought. '*Guten Tag*,' he said. 'Is this seat free?'

They did not smile or say anything, so he leaned the white cane against the seat and took off his rucksack and his coat. The woman pulled the girl to her and whispered something in her ear. The girl was called Lieschen. They watched as Willi lifted his rucksack on to the luggage rack. When they spoke to one another, which was seldom, it was in anxious whispers, and they didn't speak to Willi at all.

It was as though his blindness were contagious or dangerous. They looked elsewhere or at their hands in their laps. Only Lieschen looked at Willi. The white stick made her think he couldn't see her, so when he smiled at her, her eyes got wide and she looked away. But after a while she dared to look back and he smiled at her again. 'Lieschen,' said the woman, and pulled her closer still.

After a while Willi fell asleep, and when he woke up a different couple was sitting opposite him, a balding man with a flashy suit and a small mustache. He had his arm around a blonde woman in a fur coat and a dirndl. She had bright red lips. They both were studying him.

'At the front?' said the man, cocking his head and smiling.

Willi smiled back at him but didn't say anything.

'Going to Munich?' said the man.

Again Willi didn't speak.

'Shell-shocked, I guess,' said the man to the woman.

'I guess,' said the woman, and gave Willi what was supposed to be a sympathetic look. She adjusted her skirt to show a little more of her shapely legs, a little gift for one of Germany's sad, brave heroes.

The man saw her do it and laughed. 'You're shameless,' he said.

She laughed and kissed him, all the while with her eyes on Willi.

It was snowing a little as the train pulled into the Munich central station. The station was full of people, most of whom were not going anywhere. It was quiet except for the occasional loudspeaker announcement or the squeal of steel wheels against steel rails, and the hiss of escaping steam, as a train came to a stop. People dozed on benches or in corners away from the wind. Some stood by makeshift stoves – steel drums with fire inside – with their hands out, reaching for heat.

Willi climbed into the streetcar and took a seat reserved for invalids. He watched as large snowflakes fell on the dreary landscape. More than three years of war had drained all color from the city, or was it just his eyes? People looked lost, bewildered, half dead. And why wouldn't they, having been ground down by hunger and fear, by the death and maiming of their sons and brothers and fathers?

The war wasn't lost, according to the official line. General Ludendorff, the great German hero, was supposedly planning a massive offensive that would push the Allies into the sea. But who believed that? The streetcar rumbled from street to street, and Munich revealed itself again and again: ashen, immobile, all but unrecognizable. Everything was still here, but now it was dead, ossified, crumbling, and at an end.

There was an encampment of men in the small park behind the brick station building at the end of the line. Willi had played in that park as a boy. But now the station building was boarded up to keep the homeless out, and a cluster of tarpaper and wooden shacks had been thrown up around it. A dozen men stood by a steel drum stove.

'Hey, *Kamerad!*' one man shouted, holding up a bottle as Willi walked by. 'Come join us! Hey, *Kamerad!* I'm talking to you.'

Willi kept walking and the man lunged and grabbed him by the arm. '*Kamerad*, I'm talking to you.' Then he noticed the white stick. 'Sorry, man. C'mon, have a drink, *Kamerad*.'

'No, thanks,' said Willi. The man smelled of sweat and alcohol.

'Seriously. C'mon, *Kamerad*, have a drink,' he pushed the bottle against Willi's chest. Willi pushed it away.

'Hey, c'mon man, that's no way to treat a *Kamerad*.' He took a drink from the bottle, held it out toward Willi and gave Willi a hard look. 'Hey, I know you,' he said. 'You're Willi Geismeier, aren't you? Hey look, everybody, it's Geismeier, back from the war.' Now four of the other men came over. 'You don't remember me, Geismeier?' He leaned toward Willi again. 'Here, take a good look.'

'For Christ's sake, Karlo. He's blind.' A couple of the men laughed at that and turned back to the barrel where it was warm.

'The son of a bitch doesn't remember me,' said Karlo.

'I remember you,' said Willi.

'Yeah? So, what's my name?'

Willi turned to go.

'What's my name, Geismeier?' he said, and grabbed Willi's arm again.

'Let go of my arm,' said Willi.

'Or what?' said Karlo.

'Just let go of my arm,' said Willi.

'The son of a bitch was always too good for the likes of us, Karlo,' said the other man. Now he remembered Willi too. The rich kid. 'Just let him go. He isn't worth it.' The man steered Karlo back to the fire. 'So long . . . *Kamerad* Geismeier,' said the other man.

'So long, *Kamerad*,' Karlo shouted. 'See you at the barricades.'

HOME

Willi rang the bell and waited. Klaus Zeff, the family's caretaker for as long as Willi could remember, came out of the house. When he recognized Willi, he let out a cry and broke into a run as best he could. He unlocked and opened the gate and threw his arms around Willi.

'I wrote that I was coming,' said Willi.

'We didn't get your letter,' said Klaus. 'You're here, though. That's what matters.'

Klaus kissed Willi on both cheeks.

'Mama and Papa?' said Willi.

Having heard Klaus cry out, Willi's mother and father were waiting just inside. Klara Zeff too. And they gathered Willi into one gigantic embrace, with their sobs turning into laughter and then back again. Willi felt loved and smothered at the same time. He closed his eyes and wished they would stop.

They continued to fuss over Willi, helped him off with the rucksack, then his overcoat. Someone asked him how the trip home had been. Someone else wondered was the train crowded? How long had he been underway? Would his eyesight come back? Willi said he didn't know. Was he home for good or would he have to go back? Willi said he didn't know.

Willi asked about the men camped at the station.

'They're from the neighborhood,' said his father.

'I know,' said Willi. 'Karlo Levinski. I know.'

His father named those he knew. 'Out of work. Down on their luck,' he said. 'They're mostly harmless. They're rude. That's about it.'

Willi wanted nothing more than to be alone. 'I'd like to lie down,' he said. Their love and attention was too much to bear.

Willi's room had been closed off, so it was cold inside. Willi opened the radiator and it rattled and hissed. He stepped to the high window and looked out over the garden. Snow drifted down and settled on the iron furniture, the bare trees, the wall, the steep tile roof of the carriage house. Beside the carriage house, there was a chicken coop, built after he had left for the war and food had become scarce. Willi couldn't make out the vegetable garden but he knew there was one down there somewhere. His breath fogged up the window. He made lines in the fog with his finger. Then he wiped them away.

The familiar pictures were still on the walls – watercolors his mother had made in her youth. His diplomas from his year in England and from the Munich police academy hung side by side. His mother had put them up while he was away. His books were there – Shakespeare, his German and English dictionaries, *Brockhaus' Konversations-Lexikon* – an encyclopedia, and all his police manuals, and the notebooks full of his notes and speculations. It all seemed to be the remains of another life, familiar but having nothing to do with him now.

He picked up a Shakespeare volume and flipped through the pages. An old ticket from the Royal Shakespeare Theatre in Stratford-upon-Avon fell out and fluttered to the floor. He stared at it then left it where it lay.

Willi lay down on the bed, his hands folded behind his head. He woke up from a deep sleep three hours later to what he dreamed was gunfire but was actually the sound of his father knocking on the bedroom door.

'Sorry, son,' said his father, seeing the startled look on Willi's face. 'Come to supper. Mulli's anxious to see you.'

Mulli was Willi's grandmother. The baby Willi had heard her name Elly Mueller as Mulli, and everyone had called her Mulli ever since. Her husband, Leonhard Mueller, had died when

Willi was four. Mulli had moved into the Geismeier house for a while, but then moved back to her old apartment near the university. As a boy, Willi had loved to go there and spend the night. She kept a bed made up for him with plenty of pillows and a big down quilt. At first she would come on the streetcar to fetch him and his little suitcase, but eventually he could get there on his own. Years later, when the war started and times got hard, Mulli moved back in with his parents.

Klara Zeff had made a liver dumpling soup, an omelet with eggs from the chickens, and an assortment of roasted vegetables – leeks, cabbage, carrots, from the garden. There were great slabs of black bread. Given that people were hungry all over Munich, it was a plenteous, even luxurious meal.

'You're home,' said Mulli, not quite believing it. She touched Willi's cheek. Her fingers felt icy; Willi wanted to pull away, but he didn't. Her hair had turned white since he had last seen her. She was thinner, her skin looked like parchment now, her pale blue eyes were rimmed in red.

After dinner, Willi and his father went and sat in front of the fire. His father took a cigar from his vest pocket. It had been half smoked earlier in the day. He stuck a match and drew on the cigar until it glowed. He held it up in front of him. 'That's how it is, Willi. These days you smoke a cigar until it's done.'

Geismeier Ceramics had done a good bit of belt-tightening during the war, he said, like a lot of businesses. The Munich municipal government, their principal customer, stopped expanding the sewer system when war broke out. For a while they tried to maintain and repair the existing system, which meant they still needed the Geismeier seamless ceramic pipe, still the best and most cost-effective solution available. But soon the war was sucking up all the money that had been for roads, buildings, sewers.

The army became a customer early in the war. They were building and modernizing military bases. But that too stopped as the war had dragged on. So he had cut his own salary by half and then by half again. All the workers had agreed to pay cuts as well, as long as he kept them on the payroll, which he managed to do. On the plus side, there had been a few manufacturing innovations that would cut costs, thanks to the work of a bright young engineer he had recently hired.

'How is the business doing?' said Willi. He hadn't heard anything his father had said.

'Things are tight now,' said his father after a long pause. 'Willi, I'd like you to come work with me, to take over some of the administration. It would be good for you, get you out into the world again. I know . . .' He let his voice trail off.

'I need time, Papa. I can't see well enough to do anything right now.'

'I understand, Willi.'

'No, you don't,' said Willi. How could anyone understand?

'I know you've been through terrible things for the fatherland.' Willi stared into the fire.

'I spoke to Benno. He thinks he could find some administrative work at police headquarters . . .'

'Not now, Papa. With my eyes.'

'Is it getting better?'

'I don't know, Papa. I can't even read right now.'

'Well, I'll tell you what, Willi. Come to the office with me once you've rested up a bit, whenever you feel up to it – take your time, and I'll find something useful for you to do. Just to keep you active, you know. Just take your time.'

My time? Take my time? It doesn't work like that, thought Willi.

THE ENGINEER

Willi felt broken. He was not in the war, but the war was in him. His sleep, when it came, was filled with dreams that brought it all back. He sat alone in an empty train that never arrived anywhere. It sped through one station after another, the car rocking from side to side, the wheels clacking on the tracks. Or he was being chased through an endless trench in mud up to his knees. He was surrounded by dead and mutilated bodies and someone was crying out for help, but he couldn't find them. Or a clownish man was stuffing body parts into his mouth until Willi woke up with a start, unable to breathe.

During the day he was more or less free of the horrors, although there was an emptiness where he had once imagined his soul resided. He tried to read his beloved Shakespeare – he had the complete works in English and in the August Wilhelm Schlegel translation. But the war had changed Shakespeare's dramas too, whether tragedy or comedy, into a catalogue of horrors – cruelty, malevolence, greed, insane ambition.

Some men appeared somehow to be able to remove themselves from what they had lived through, what had been done to them, and what they had done to others. They pulled themselves together, got back to the lives they had left behind, took up old occupations and habits, found something that at least resembled happiness.

But then there were the others, like Karlo Levinski, who had accosted Willi at the station, whose ruination was thorough and complete. Karlo had been in the trenches for two months, almost all of it under nearly constant attack from French mortars. *Only* two months. Except, as most men who had been there would tell you, time does not exist in hell. Two months or two years: it is all eternity.

Karlo waded in mud and offal and excrement night and day. The almost constant thump of mortars was followed by the howl and whistle of incoming shells. Then a shower of mud and gore rained down all around and the screaming started. The screaming wouldn't stop. And sometimes Karlo realized he was the one screaming. At night, when Karlo was standing guard duty, flares cast the ragged, ruined landscape in garish tones of black and yellow. Shadows shifted sideways as the flare fell, and then the attack came.

Day after day, Karlo went a little crazier. One night after a mortar attack, the flares were up and the sergeant ordered his squad over the top. They scrambled up the ladder and were cut down by machine-gun fire immediately. And Karlo, who was supposed to be the last to go, put his rifle against his own foot and fired without even thinking, and then, just to be certain, he fired again.

Karlo was dragged by the arms back to the field hospital. The soldiers who took him took turns cursing and punching him for being a coward. 'You bastard. What about the rest of us stuck out here?' 'D'you ever think of that?' 'You rotten son of a bitch.'

All the other men in the ward, blinded or with limbs missing or other grievous injuries, knew he was a coward too. They menaced and threatened him, promising to kill him, if the army didn't do it for them.

Then Karlo got lucky. The captain assigned to judge him had just lost his own son to a firing squad. The boy had done more or less the same thing Karlo had done, except he had chopped off the fingers of one hand. He had been tried for treason and had been executed two hours later.

The captain tried Karlo while he was lying in his hospital bed. The men all around were jeering and the captain ordered them all to be silent. The captain wanted to be just, but all he could see in Karlo was another damaged boy. He gave Karlo eighteen months in prison and a dishonorable discharge from the army.

Willi learned that some veterans got together in a Gasthaus a few blocks away between the post office and a shuttered grocery store. He walked over one afternoon. The Gasthaus zum Löwen had a bar and several small tables. The tables had been pushed together and about a dozen young men in various states of disrepair sat around them. There was one other white cane, two men with crutches. Others were missing limbs, still others had wounds you couldn't see. Any man who was able was still at the front. Willi didn't know any of them. They all shook hands, welcomed him, and put a beer in front of him.

Willi said he was back from Ypres after nearly three years out there. One other man, Avraham, had been at Ypres too. He made a joke about how when the gas settled into the trenches, your only choice was to stick your head up so some sniper could shoot it off. Another guy said something about the numbers of reinforcements being sent out.

'Yeah,' said still another guy. 'The fatherland will emerge victorious.'

The first guy said that was all shit. They were sending schoolboys to fight.

Then the fatherland-guy said that was defeatism, treachery. It was their military duty now to secure the home front, to help keep morale up until victory was theirs.

'Are you kidding? Our duty is to stop this war and see it never happens again.'

'Look to Russia,' said Avraham. 'Look what's going on there, comrades. The czar is gone, the revolution has started.'

'We need to fight for a better future.' They tried to talk about the better future, but no one could agree on what that might look like. The conversation became an argument, and then circled back to the past. What had gone wrong, who was killing Germany. Willi left early and never went back.

Willi sat on the old iron bench in the garden some days. He listened to the birds or just watched the clouds pass. One morning he heard a feeble squeak that he thought was a bird, but when he looked he saw a kitten, orange, starving, bedraggled, with infected, runny eyes, and so tiny that when he picked it up he could hold it in the palm of his hand. The kitten trembled and cried.

Willi put the kitten inside his jacket and went inside. He warmed a little milk, put it in a cup, put his finger in the milk, and held it up to the kitten's nose. It opened its mouth and chewed the milk off Willi's finger as though it were nursing. Willi named the kitten Puck.

Willi's mother and father had never had animals and didn't like one in the house. His mother claimed to be allergic, but it turned out she wasn't. Willi got some eye drops and swabbed Puck's eyes with cotton. He put aside a little food from every meal – cheese, beans, eggs, greens, it didn't matter – mashed it up, and fed it to Puck. And Puck ate everything.

When Willi was at home, Puck didn't let him out of his sight, following him from room to room, sleeping with him at night, sitting with him when he read, watching birds with him in the garden, and growing bigger and stronger all the time.

One evening Willi went to his father sitting by the fire. The old man – he looked old in a way Willi hadn't noticed before – looked up in surprise. 'I'll go to work with you tomorrow. If you'd still like me to.'

'If you're ready,' said his father. He held his hand out toward Willi and, after a long time, Willi took it.

'I don't know if I am,' said Willi. 'But I'm ready for something other than waiting to be fine.'

A car picked them up at seven. Puck sat in the window and watched them go. 'He'll be back,' said Willi's mother, and petted Puck. She understood that Puck had saved Willi's life.

The car dropped Willi and his father at the factory entrance. They hung their coats in the cloakroom and walked down to the factory floor. Willi had known some of the workers before the war, some of the old-timers from even earlier when he had been a boy. They all shook his hand and welcomed him. They said they were pleased to see him. Would he be working here now? Willi said he thought he would. For a while. They nodded and said, 'Yes, yes. Of course.' Upstairs in the offices he saw clerks and secretaries he had known, and it went the same way. Everyone was polite and friendly with the boss's son.

'Eva,' said Willi's father, 'this is my son, Willi. Willi, this is Eva Berlot, the engineer I mentioned, who's doing such good work for us.' Willi and Eva shook hands.

'So you're just back,' said Eva.

'Yes,' said Willi.

'You must be glad to be home,' she said.

'Yes, I am,' said Willi. Then he couldn't think of anything more to say.

Attraction is like that, especially when it comes so unexpectedly, amidst a vast indifference and sorrow, like a flower in a desert, as it did now for Willi. It can stymie us. It puts a stop to words. Willi was startled by the look of Eva, though you or I might not be. But he saw something with such clarity that he had to wonder if his diminished sight had suddenly been restored.

He stood there, tall, his arms dangling at his side, his eyes wide behind the thick glasses. A smile crept across his mouth. He wondered whether the unfamiliar gesture might cause his face to crack and fall off.

Eva felt that she saw the goodness of this man. She had never seen him before, but she felt she had always known him.

'Well, Eva,' said Willi's father, who had noticed it all, 'I know you're busy. Don't let us keep you.'

'Yes, thank you,' said Eva. Willi gave her his hand again. 'Nice to meet you,' she said, and walked off down the hall. Willi tried not to watch her go.

Willi was given a desk and the task of writing proposals bidding on new jobs. He read old proposals – he had to hold them right in front of his glasses and read word by word – to learn the format and the language of proposals, and then he wrote a couple of proposals himself. He was good at it, but the work meant nothing to him.

At noon, he went down to the canteen for lunch. You got a tray and went through the line, where you were given a bowl of pea soup with a sausage, boiled potatoes, kraut and a mug of beer. Willi sat down at one of the long tables. He saw Eva coming toward him and quickly looked down, pretending to concentrate on eating.

Eva sat down with some men who Willi guessed were from the engineering department. They were near enough that he could hear their voices and their laughter but not what was being said. Afterwards, as he was passing his tray through the window to the dishwashers, Eva came up beside him. She slid her tray through the window too. 'How was your lunch?' she said.

'Very good,' he said. 'And yours?'

'Not every factory has a canteen like this,' she said.

'No,' said Willi.

'I would have joined you,' she said. 'But it looked like you wanted to be alone.'

'No, I didn't,' he said. 'No. Not at all.'

'Well,' she said. 'Maybe tomorrow.'

'Yes, tomorrow,' he said.

That night he said, 'Puck, I am a complete idiot.'

KARLO'S FRIENDS

After that first day, Willi decided to take the streetcar to work. He felt uncomfortable arriving in a private car. After a few more days, he asked his father whether he could move downstairs to the factory. He wanted physical work,

work that would exhaust him, allow him to sleep through the night.

Willi reported to Heinz Fritsch, the warehouse foreman. Heinz put him to work shoveling clay from the railroad hoppers into smaller hoppers, that he then wheeled into the factory. There he dumped the clay on to a conveyor that carried it up to the grinders and processors.

After processing, it went by conveyor to be packed into molds. The molds were stacked in the drying room until the dried clay, now shaped into sections of pipe, could be extracted. Then they were allowed to dry some more. Once the pipe sections were properly dried, they were lowered into the glazing vats, and from there they went straight to the kilns. After baking they were transported to the cooling hall, and then out the other side where they were crated and loaded into freight cars or trucks for delivery.

Willi and Eva ate lunch together most days. He would come in from the warehouse, his coveralls and boots gray from the clay.

'It's heavy work,' said Eva. 'Do you like it?'

'Yes,' said Willi. 'It's good for me.'

Eva asked whether he noticed ways the process might be improved. Willi's father had brought her in to update the manufacturing process to take advantage of the newest innovations in automation. The trick, she said, was to improve efficiency without sacrificing quality. Willi thought some power implements that could transfer clay from the railroad hoppers to the factory hoppers would be real labor savers. Eva said she had heard that from other workers and had been working on something like that for the last months – pneumatic scraping blades suspended from tracks on the ceiling. She thought they would have a prototype to try out before too long.

Eva had grown up in Straßburg, which had been German for the last fifty years. Before that it had been French. And soon, once the war was lost, it would be French again. She was the first female engineering student in the history of the University of Straßburg, then known as the Kaiser Wilhelm University.

'How did you get interested in engineering?' said Willi.

'I've always liked to know how things worked,' said Eva. 'I took stuff apart as a kid. Clocks, a typewriter, other machines. Sometimes I even managed to put them back together.' She laughed, which sounded like bells. 'My father said I should be an engineer. He was joking the first time he said it. But I liked the idea, and he came to like it too.'

'Is it hard being the only woman in a profession?'

'A little. The professors in Straßburg didn't like having a girl in the seminars, in their man's world. And the boys liked to show off that they were smarter than I was. Except it turned out they weren't.'

Willi told her that he had been a detective before the war.

'You must have been one of Munich's youngest,' she said.

'Yes,' he said.

He said he had liked the work. Eva asked what he had liked about it. He said he imagined it was pretty much the same thing she said about engineering: discovering how things worked. Although in the case of police work, unlike engineering, it was people and not machines or bridges. And by the time a detective got ahold of it, things had pretty much come apart already. So the detective's job was to figure out how and why that had happened, how the parts all fit together. So that things – society – could be put back together. Crime was a disruption of the natural order, he said. Like war.

Later in life – after he had lived through the depression, lived through life in Hitler's Germany, lived through yet another war, and further depredations, 'the heart-ache and thousand natural shocks that flesh is heir to,' he came to believe that chaos was more or less the natural order of things, and a decent and lawful society was an unnatural and at best temporary interlude before the world reverted yet again to its norm, which was chaos.

'Do you think you'll go back to being a detective?'

'I don't know if I can,' said Willi.

'But do you want to?' said Eva.

'I don't know that either,' said Willi.

'Why not?' said Eva.

'Well, my eyesight, for one thing.'

'That's not it, though, is it?'

'No,' said Willi. She waited. 'It's my brain,' he said. 'It's a different brain than I used to have. It's . . . damaged.'

'What do you mean?'

'It seems to work all right, but there's a kind of fog now between me and the world. It's like a constant background noise. I don't hear it, but I feel it, I know it's there.' He realized later that he had been trying to let her know what she was getting into, maybe to warn her off. But she just said, 'That's interesting.'

Willi and Eva had just finished lunch one Friday when two men approached and asked if he was Willi Geismeier. He said he was. They said they were policemen. They showed him badges, and said they wanted a word with him. The canteen was pretty much empty by now. So Eva excused herself, and the two men took off their hats and sat down opposite Willi.

'Do you know someone named Karlo Levinsky?' said the older of the two.

'I used to know him,' said Willi.

'But you don't know him any longer?'

'Not really.'

'Have you seen him lately?'

'Yes, I have.'

'When was that?'

'The afternoon of the ninth of January.'

'And you remember the exact date and time, just like that?' said the younger one.

'It was the day I got home from the war. That's why I remember it.'

'And where did you see him?' said the older one.

'On my way home from the train station. There is an encampment of homeless men by the station. He was there. He called out to me.'

'An *encampment*,' said the younger one and looked meaningfully at the older one. 'You haven't asked us why we're asking,' he said.

'No,' said Willi.

'Why's that?' said the younger one.

'Why should I?' said Willi.

The two men looked at each other.

'OK, Geismeier,' said the older one, as though now things were going to get serious. 'What's your relationship with *Kamerad* Levinsky?'

'I don't have a relationship with him,' said Willi.

'He says otherwise,' said the younger one.

'He says you assaulted him,' said the older one.

'That's not true,' said Willi. 'I didn't assault him.'

'He's got the injuries to prove it,' said the younger one. 'Concussion, broken fingers, bruises.'

'Are you serious?' said Willi. 'His injuries don't prove I did anything.'

'You don't sound surprised or upset about his injuries,' said the older one.

Willi didn't respond.

'So what was your last meeting with Karlo Levinski like?' said the older one.

'I was on my way home that day, and he called out to me, and I tried to ignore him. He wasn't happy that I passed him by without speaking. He grabbed me. I told him to stop, he swore at me, and that was the end of it.'

'He called you *Kamerad*,' said the younger one.

'Yes, that's right. So what?' said Willi.

'Weren't you offended?'

'Why? To be called *Kamerad*?' said Willi.

'Yes, *Kamerad*,' said the older one, trying to goad him to prove the point.

'I don't think of us as comrades,' said Willi. 'But, no, I wasn't offended.'

'You aren't comrades? He served like you did, *Kamerad*,' said the older one, still looking for a reaction.

Willi stood up. 'You're not here as cops, are you?' he said.

Now the two men stood up. 'What do you mean?' said the older one.

'Let me see your badges again,' said Willi.

'Why?' said the younger one.

'I want to see the numbers,' said Willi. 'What are your names?'

The two men looked at each other. 'Let's go,' said the older one. The two men put on their hats.

'We'll meet again, Geismeier,' said the younger one.

* * *

Karlo Levinsky wasn't living in the encampment any more. He slept on a sofa in his mother's small basement apartment, and that was where Willi found him. Karlo's head was wrapped in a gauze bandage. A little blood had seeped through. His face was bruised and his hair was matted. He tried to sit up as his mother showed Willi into the room.

'What the hell do you want?' said Karlo.

'Hello, Karlo,' said Willi.

'I said, what are you doing here?'

'What happened to you?'

'As if you didn't know. I swear you'll never sucker me like that again.'

'Yeah. I guess you're not that tough, if even a blind man can do that kind of damage.'

'Go to hell, you asshole,' said Karlo.

'So tell me what you think happened.'

'You know damn well what happened. You pushed me down the stairs.'

'Where did this happen?'

'Stop playing games, Geismeier.'

'And you're sure it was me?'

'You're damn right it was you, you bastard.'

'You saw me do it.'

'You're damn right I did.'

'You saw me push you. Did I push you with one hand or two?'

'How should I know?'

'Was I waiting for you there, at the station?'

'How should I know?'

'So you didn't see me.'

'Oh, I saw you, you bastard, and I'm going to—'

'So you must have described it to the cops. So what did you tell them?'

Karlo laughed. 'That's where you're wrong, Geismeier. I didn't have to. They *saw* the whole thing. They were right there when you did it. The cops saw it all.'

'Do you know their names?'

'Waldheim and Geier. They saw it all.'

'And they told you what happened, told you it was me? So, you didn't see it, did you? Waldheim and Geier saw it and told you.'

'Same thing,' said Karlo.

'Are you friends with Waldheim and Geier?'

'What's it to you?' said Karlo.

'Are they your political comrades?' said Willi.

'That's none of your business, either,' said Karlo. 'But for your information, yeah, they're part of the struggle to save Germany from the communists and the Jews.'

'And, let me guess, Karlo: you're having doubts.'

'So what?'

'Maybe you were pushed because you're having doubts.'

'What are you talking about, Geismeier? Anyway, why would they lie?'

'That's the question right there, isn't it, Karlo? Why would they lie?'

DETECTIVE GEISMEIER

The next day Willi began putting together his application to rejoin the police and to take the detective examinations. Willi's application had strong supporting letters. There was one from his father's friend Benno von Horvath who was a police chief. And there was one from Robert Oberhof, who was now a detective captain. Oberhof gave Willi full credit for having unraveled the Walther Metzger murder three years earlier. Arenz was serving twenty-five years, Oberhof had been promoted, and the case was now studied in the police academy.

'Are you up to it, Geismeier?' said the police captain whose job it was to make the final determination. He had read the medical report and the army discharge papers.

'I'm fine, Captain.' Willi was strong and fit, thanks to the two months of heavy labor at Geismeier Ceramics. And he no longer needed the white cane.

'What about your eyes?'

'They're pretty good,' said Willi, 'thanks to these.' He touched his glasses.

The captain looked at him doubtfully. 'Well, you're going to have to pass an eye exam,' he said.

Willi was able to pass just barely, thanks to a couple of good guesses.

'So you're leaving,' said Eva.

'Leaving Geismeier Ceramics,' he said.

'Yes. But still.'

'I'm not leaving you,' he said.

She reached across the table and touched his hand. He said he would come by the canteen for lunch as often as he could. He said they could take the train to the mountains, go hiking, go swimming in the Bavarian lakes, now that spring had come and the weather was getting warmer. The war was still raging, but it was far away. The trees in the English Garden were draped in tender green leaves, tulips were in bloom, the fruit trees had blossoms. He told his mother and father that he and Eva were in love and he wanted to marry her.

His father said all the things fathers say to their sons when they say they're in love. He liked Eva very much, she was a good person, and, yes, she was very pretty. But Willi should give himself time. He and Eva should get to know each other better. Willi was still young; he shouldn't rush into anything. Willi tried to reassure his parents that he wasn't rushing into anything, but young people never think they're rushing into anything.

On passing the detective exam, Willi was assigned to a precinct in the Ludwigsvorstadt. Precinct headquarters were in a brick building at the back of a courtyard on Schillerstraße, a few hundred meters south of the central train station, and just to the west of the old city center. Willi knocked on Sergeant Ove Sandheim's door. 'Just go in,' said the policeman sitting nearby. 'He's hard of hearing.'

Willi went in. 'Detective Willi Geismeier reporting for duty, Sergeant.'

Sandheim cupped his hand behind his ear. 'Say it again,' he said.

Willi did, and the sergeant stood up, and the two men shook hands.

'Welcome, Detective,' he said.

'Thank you, Sergeant,' said Willi.

'Are you political, Geismeier?'

'Political? No, Sergeant,' said Willi.

'No revolution, no Munich commune? No bring back the king, none of that shit?'

'No, Sergeant.'

'Good. I don't stand for any of that stuff here. This is a police station.'

Ove took Willi around the station and introduced him to the other patrolmen and detectives. There was no one Willi knew. His new partner, Ludwig Voss, peered at him over his glasses. Ludwig had close-cropped white hair and an upswept mustache like the Kaiser's. They shook hands and he handed Willi a small stack of case files and the Standard Procedures handbook. 'Ove will quiz you on that,' he said, tapping the handbook. 'He's a stickler for procedure. Everything by the book.'

At twelve Ludwig said, 'Let's go to lunch.' They went to the Gasthaus around the corner. It should have been filled with workmen at this hour, but most of the tables were empty. There had been street violence in the neighborhood – communists against fascists. And now there was this so-called *Spanische Grippe*, the Spanish flu. 'People are scared,' said Ludwig, 'but it probably won't amount to anything.'

The waitress brought their food. Willi had sausage, potatoes, kraut, and beer; Ludwig had liver dumpling soup.

'You know, I'm on my way out, Willi,' said Ludwig. 'I'm retiring at the end of the year.'

'Really? Why?' said Willi.

Ludwig smiled. 'Don't take it personally, but I have grandchildren your age. I put in my papers long before you showed up.'

Willi told Ludwig about Waldheim and Geier.

'You should deal with that before you do anything else,' said Ludwig.

Because they were policemen, Willi found them easily. He talked to their colleagues and learned they had both left the police recently to join one of the nationalist militias. Waldheim had already been a militiaman. Geier and his friend Karlo started going to rallies and soon joined up. But now Karlo was suspected by Lieutenant Wedekind, the head of the militia, of being a communist spy. 'He has to be dealt with,' said Wedekind. Waldheim said he and Geier would do it, but he proposed they make it look like Geismeier had done it and he could take the fall. He already had a history with Karlo, so he was a plausible suspect.

Willi found the two men in the bar they frequented. Geier, the younger one, recognized Willi and stood up. 'Look who's here,' he said.

Willi held up his badge in front of their faces, which surprised them a little.

'So what can we do for you, *Kamerad?*' said Waldheim.

'I have a few questions about your assault on Karlo Levinski,' said Willi.

'That wasn't us, *Kamerad*,' said Waldheim. He just couldn't leave the '*Kamerad*' thing alone.

'You can't prove anything,' said Geier.

'Shut up, Geier,' said Waldheim. 'He's just fishing.'

It was true that Willi was fishing. But once he persuaded first Geier then Waldheim that Karlo was ready to testify that they had pushed him, and that some of their former fellow police officers knew about the attack and would testify, and that even one of their militia comrades had singled them out as the ones tasked with settling the score, each was eager to implicate the other.

Willi interrupted them to explain that they should both expect to be charged with assault and battery, and with impersonating police officers.

'We *were* police officers,' said Geier.

'Not when you showed me your badges,' said Willi.

However, as Ove explained, all Willi could do under the latest policing regime was refer the case to the precinct in which the crimes had been committed, and hope that they would be charged.

Meanwhile, Ludwig said he had a case that had been giving him fits. 'I'm not even sure it's a case,' he said. He dropped a thick file on Willi's desk. 'Take a look.' Willi said he would, but he didn't get the chance.

THE PLAGUE

I n the spring of 1918 in the third battle of the Aisne, the Germans pushed the Allies back through France and advanced the lines to within sixty kilometers of Paris. It was a bloody and hard-fought battle, an unexpected victory for the Germans, and they took many prisoners.

Before long, German soldiers started falling ill and dying. What came to be called *die Spanische Grippe* spread rapidly through the army, and the soldiers going home on leave or discharged because of injuries carried it to every corner of Germany. As word of the sickness and the sickness itself spread across the country, the supposition was that either the Black Plague had returned or that the enemy was using germ warfare. But it wasn't the plague.

Soldiers and civilians on both sides were getting sick and dying, so it wasn't germ warfare either. A bewildering variety of symptoms came over you suddenly – a smothering wave of weakness, dizziness, high fever, coughing. You vomited or couldn't get enough air, or both. A body might take on a bluish hue from a lack of oxygen. Sometimes blood ran from your eyes or ears. The infection killed by filling your lungs with fluid, essentially drowning you. Those it didn't kill right away became vulnerable to infections that finished the job.

There was no remedy. Doctors and scientists were left to their own devices, trying to discover the cause of this deadly and widespread infection. Laboratories worked on vaccines against the Pfeiffer bacillus, which many scientists thought the most likely cause. They improvised treatments of every variety, repurposing existing medications and methodologies. But there was little anyone was able to do to cure it or stop its spread.

People were ordered to wear masks, to observe good personal hygiene. They were told to isolate, to get as much fresh air as possible. Some of the recommendations issued may have been helpful, others were just acts of desperation. Doctors tried intubating their suffocating patients and then pumping air into their lungs, but that did more harm than good. They treated patients with quinine, mercury chloride, creosote and countless other untested, unproven and often harmful remedies. Nothing they tried helped.

Hospitals filled up with the sick and dying. Like other cities, Munich opened provisional clinics in gymnasiums, banks, and whatever space they could find. But there was soon a severe shortage of physicians and nurses. They too were falling sick and dying in staggering numbers. Volunteers were called for, but of course very few people volunteered for what was likely a death sentence.

This terrible new plague, and the panic, which spread even more quickly than the fever, brought out thieves and swindlers, They advertised remedies and cures that promised certain protection from infection or certain cure once you were infected. Desperation drove people to believe everything and try anything.

Insurance companies appeared with impressive names like German Mutual or Munich Independent Life, offering policies that promised to pay for your treatment or pay your family if, heaven forbid, you died. The company names in florid typefaces on impressive prospectuses were invented, the seals and signatures at the bottom of the policy papers were fake. When you mailed in your claim, it came back as undeliverable.

Eva had been working on an air-filtration system to reduce the clay dust circulating in the Geismeier Ceramics workshop, and now she set about adapting her ideas so they might be used in hospitals and clinics. She set up meetings with city officials and engineers at the Ludwig Maximilian University hospital to offer them her services. She was on the streetcar on her way to one such meeting when her vision suddenly went foggy and she couldn't catch her breath. She collapsed on to the floor of the streetcar and was carried into the nearby hospital.

Willi went to the hospital as soon as he heard. She had a high fever and was struggling to breathe. The doctors and nurses were overwhelmed by the flood of new patients, and there was nothing they could do for her. So Willi took over her care, which amounted to putting damp towels on her forehead, helping her sip water, and mostly holding her hand. Eva was delirious or sleeping. Willi studied her face, still so new to him, but already so familiar. Her breathing was shallow. Sometimes her eyes flickered open, but they did not recognize him and the lids fell closed like a curtain coming down.

The hospital wards were filled beyond capacity. The hallways were lined with cots. Except for a long, barking cough, as someone nearby tried to get enough air, the hospital was strangely quiet. When anyone spoke – doctors or nurses or patients or their families – it was in hushed whispers, as though they knew they were in the presence of a great evil which they did not want to further upset.

After two days at Eva's bedside, Willi fell ill. The disease was everywhere now.

Willi lay in bed in a men's ward. He was bathed in sweat, his head was throbbing, his throat was burning and raw. As he slipped into unconsciousness, it was like going down a long trench lit by exploding flares. His heart was racing, his chest heaving, he felt himself reaching, searching for oxygen. It was like the gas attacks he had lived through all over again. He imagined himself wrestling an inadequate gas mask into place over his nose and mouth. He tasted blood. The heat was tremendous. A constant roar filled his ears, stopping all other sound, like an explosion that would not stop.

Willi regained consciousness after three days. An old man sat beside him holding a cup of water to his lips. 'There you are,' said the old man. 'The war is over,' he said. While Willi had been unconscious, the Kaiser had abdicated and fled to Holland.

Willi finally saw that the old man was his father. He tried to speak, but the effort was more than he could manage. He couldn't turn his head or lift his arm. They were in a vast hall with row upon row of cots, each one occupied, and each one separated from all the others by curtains. Masked nurses and doctors passed through the narrow aisles in silence, doing what they could – which wasn't much – for the hundreds of men lying there. If you had someone with you, as Willi did, you didn't need them and they passed you by.

THE ROYAL BAVARIAN ASSURANCE COMPANY

Two days later Willi's father came in a car and drove him home. Willi spent the next weeks in bed, at first drifting in and out of consciousness, then too weak to do any more than lift his head so that his mother could feed him. Doctor Trevelius came every day and took Willi's temperature. He thumped Willi's chest with his knuckles and listened to his lungs. 'It's getting clearer,' he said. 'Better.'

Puck slept on the pillow beside Willi's head. Doctor Trevelius didn't approve, but Willi's mother said Puck had saved him once before, and maybe he could do it again.

Eva had been buried before Willi even knew she was dead. She had died alone in a women's ward. Willi had already been a witness to more death than most of us will see in a lifetime. But Eva was his first love, so this was a death of an entirely different order, surprisingly large and profoundly sharp. He felt something like a stab to his chest when his father told him.

So this is what a broken heart feels like. Tears spilled down his cheeks. The *Spanische Grippe* was highly contagious, his father said, and so the dead had to be buried as quickly as possible.

'Where is she buried?' said Willi. His father told him.

Willi's mother and father sat with the doctor, drinking tea and brandy. 'Not much is known about this *Grippe*,' said Trevelius. 'Not what causes it, and not what to do for it. The suspicion is it's a bacterium, but I don't know any more than that.

'Yes, I think Willi will recover. But his system is very depleted. He has lost ten kilos, and he was already thin to begin with.' You could count his ribs and see his entire backbone. 'Make sure he gets lots of iron, eats lots of liver, kidneys; organ meat is the best thing for him. Make sure he moves his bowels regularly.'

After ten days or so, Willi started eating solid food. Finally the doctor told him he could return to active life whenever he felt up to it.

'Active life?' said Willi.

'Work, if you like,' said Trevelius.

One day a thick envelope came for Willi from Pierre Berlot in Straßburg.

> *Dear Herr Geismeier,*
>
> *We hope you are well. Our dear Eva wrote us that you are a fine man and that she was in love with you and wanted to marry you. Now God has taken her from us and from you, and all we have left is grief and the knowledge that His plan for our beloved Eva surpasses our understanding. We are desolate but confident in His wisdom.*
>
> *During the early days of the terrible plague consuming the world, Eva purchased a life insurance policy from the Royal Bavarian Assurance Company with a value of ten thousand Reichsmarks in which she named us as beneficiaries.*
>
> *We have tried, without success, to cash in the policy. We have written the company multiple times and have not heard back. We have enclosed a copy of the policy with the pertinent information. Could you please contact the appropriate authorities and see why the payment has not been forthcoming?*
>
> *Thank you in advance for your kind help.*
>
> *Yours sincerely, in God's name,*
>
> *Pierre and Marie Berlot*

At the top of the enclosed insurance policy was ROYAL BAVARIAN ASSURANCE CO., followed by a Munich Post Office box number. The document had pages of insurance boiler plate, with many 'whereases' and references like 'Royal Bavarian Assurance, herein referred to as "the Company" and the "insured party herein named."'

Nowhere in the document was there a street address or telephone number or other contact information. Claims could be filed, it was stated, by sending proof of death of the insured party

herein named to 'the Company' at the above given post office
box.

The desk sergeant didn't recognize Willi when he came through
the station door. He looked like an old man, shrunken, skeletal,
and leaning on a cane. Ove Sandheim, the chief sergeant, had
the same reaction, and then so did Ludwig Voss, Willi's partner.
'Christ, Geismeier, you look older than me. What the hell are
you doing here? You should be home in bed.'

Willi said he was only there on a personal matter. To help
Eva's parents collect on her insurance policy, he wanted to find
an address for the Royal Bavarian Assurance Company. There
had to be a record somewhere of the company's physical
address and the principals involved, the executives and owners.
Willi sat slumped at his desk while Ludwig went to get the
Münchener Unternehmensregister, the Munich Company
Register, a thick binder that was updated monthly with new
pages. Royal Bavarian Assurance was not listed in the main
volume or in the updates.

'You want me to call the post office?' said Ludwig. 'They
won't want to say who owns the box. But if we need to, we can
try for a court order.'

'I'll call,' said Willi.

Just as Ludwig had predicted, the post office declined to help.
The man on the phone said the names of the owners of boxes
was privileged information that could not be given out.

'This is a police matter,' said Willi.

The man on the phone was not impressed.

'What's your name, sir?' said Willi. When the man declined
to give it, Willi said, 'I'll need it for the court order.'

'Doctor Hildesheim, postal inspector,' said the man.

'Doctor Hildesheim,' said Willi, 'as I already explained, I am
asking you for the name of the owner of this post-office box as
part of a police investigation. We have good reason to believe
that the owners of that box are using it to commit insurance
fraud. If you force me to get a court order, we will petition for
an order revealing the owners of every single box in Munich. It
is the only way we can make certain this particular box is the
only one these criminals are using.'

Willi waited while Hildesheim considered his options. Finally he said, 'Blau-Weiß Printing Company.'

'Address?' said Willi.

'29 Lauensteinstraße.'

'Thank you, Herr Doctor, for your cooperation.' Willi hung up the phone.

Ludwig laughed. 'There's no way you were ever going to get that court order.'

'I know,' said Willi.

After telling Ove about what looked like a case of insurance fraud, Willi took the streetcar home. The ruined station where Karlo and his comrades had been camped was boarded up and papered over with posters. One showed Kaiser Wilhelm with a red X across his face. Another showed a map of Germany with a sword sticking out. STAB IN THE BACK, it said. A hammer and sickle had been painted across one wall.

Willi's mother watched from the window while he struggled with the heavy gate and shuffled up the garden path leaning on his cane. He wanted to go straight up to his room and get in bed, but his mother made him eat first – liver, roasted potatoes, turnips, kraut.

'He is running on empty,' said his father once he had limped upstairs.

'The war, the *Grippe*, and now Eva, it's too much for any human,' said his mother. 'It has taken the life out of him.'

A few days later, Willi's mother fell ill and his father the day after that. Doctor Trevelius came, but all he could do was shrug helplessly. 'There are chains of sickness,' he said, 'where it passes through a family like this.' He spread his hands in a sign of resignation.

Now Willi sat with his parents, fed them, talked to them, held their hands. His father didn't stop coughing until the moment he died. His mother died silently a short while later. They were buried in the Geismeier family plot in the Nordfriedhof, the North Cemetery.

Willi stood at their grave, leaning on his cane, while a Lutheran minister spoke in vague words about how beloved they were, what good people they were. Willi wondered whether the man had even known them. The Zepps were there with their daughter,

Lola. She had come home for the funeral. Many of the men and women from Geismeier Ceramics were there as well. When the ceremony was over and the graves were being closed, everyone passed by Willi and offered condolences, wondering as they did, what would become of Geismeier Ceramics, how long would they still have jobs.

Lola walked Willi home, her arm in his. Lola had gotten pregnant at seventeen, had married, had lost the child, had then lost her husband, shot through the eye by a sniper in Belgium. It had been six months before Lola found out he was dead. She had worked in a field hospital and now worked as a private nurse in Augsburg. With everything that had happened to them both, they would have had lots to talk about. Still, they walked in silence.

THE BRIDGE

When the will was settled, Willi's parents had left Lola's parents enough money to live comfortably. They moved to a small house on the far outskirts of the city, from where, on a clear day, they could see the Alps shimmering white in the distance.

Willi's father had always said he would leave Geismeier Ceramics to his employees, and he did just that. As instructed, the lawyer held a series of meetings with the new owners and helped them organize the company into a cooperative. Heinz Fritsch had been there longer than anyone else and had already been serving as the president's assistant for the last months. His fellow employees now chose him to be the new president of the company.

At a memorial gathering at Geismeier Ceramics, Heinz made a speech describing the company as a special place to work, and vowing that it would remain so as long as he was president. The employees had voted to name Willi honorary chairman. Heinz Fritsch shook Willi's hand and asked him to unveil the portrait they had commissioned of his father. Willi pulled on the golden rope and the black velvet curtain fell to the floor. There, in a gilt frame, was his father in a dark suit, seated on his favorite chair, a cigar in his hand, the familiar half-smile on his face. The painting was hung in the factory's entry hall. Geismeier Ceramics continued for eleven more years as a bastion of decency and productivity while German society came apart around it.

What started as a mutiny by sailors in Kiel in the far north, exploded into a full-blown revolution and spread across Germany like the plague. The National Assembly organized a republican government as quickly as they could to fill the void. They signed an armistice to stop the war. Even though an armistice had been urged on them by the military high command, they were now accused by the same high command of betrayal, of stabbing Germany in the back.

In Munich, the socialist Kurt Eisner seized power from the Bavarian King Ludwig the Third and declared Bavaria a free state. 'Can he do that?' said Count Sigismund Maria von Wittelsbach. The count had survived the war, although his horse Abendstern had not. The count, crippled by arthritis and suffering from the beginnings of dementia, was hustled into a car by his Austrian nephew and driven to Salzburg. 'Where are we going?' he wondered aloud. 'Will there be horses?' There were horses, but the count was in no condition to ride.

Within four months the new premier, Kurt Eisner, had taken two bullets to the brain at point-blank range. His assassin Count Anton Arco-Valley had waited in the entry to the foreign ministry and attacked Eisner from behind.

'Arco-Valley?' said the count, lowering his newspaper. 'I know that name. Didn't he serve?'

'The Royal Bavarian Infantry,' said the count's nephew.

'Infantry? So,' said the count, 'not cavalry then?' After a long pause the count said, 'And Eisner? A Jew, wasn't he?'

'Yes,' said the nephew.

'So that was it, then, was it?' said the count. 'But he was upstanding, I think.'

'Yes, I think he was,' said the nephew. 'A decent man.'

The communists rallied to establish a Bavarian Socialist Republic, which they did, and which collapsed just as quickly under violent attack by roving bands of army veterans, many like

Arco-Valley, clinging to lies about a colossal betrayal of
Germany's greatness by Jews, republicans, socialists and communists. There were barricades and checkpoints in the streets, parts
of the city were controlled by the communists and parts by the
Freikorps, the fascist militias. Munich was riven by violence,
shortages, hunger, and of course still the *Spanische Grippe*.

Willi's physical strength was returning. But an endless loop of
sorrow and despair circled through his brain, trying to convince
him in a hundred ways that life on earth was not worth living.
It was little more than madness and darkness, sickness and
misery. Those he loved were dead. One terrible war had just
ended, another was surely on its way.

When Willi tried to argue his way out of it, all he came up
with was platitudes – *life goes on; someday I will love again;
the world will heal; Germans are more decent than this* – which
only made his despair more profound. Every evening Puck was
watching by the window for him to come home and followed
him from room to room when he was there. But they didn't talk
much any more.

The big house was Willi's now, and for the time being he left
it as it was. He lived only in the kitchen, the sitting room with
the fireplace where his father had loved to smoke his cigar, and
in his bedroom upstairs. One day he gathered his parents' clothes
together. He could smell his mother's lavender water, his father's
cigars as he carried them downstairs. He found a charity at St
Martin's Church that would give them to the needy.

Willi opened the gate and a truck backed up to the house. The
two men, who carried out armfuls of clothes, were themselves
shabbily dressed. 'What about the furniture?' said one, looking
around. 'Any of that going?'

'No,' said Willi. 'Not yet.'

'OK,' said the man. You could hear the disappointment in
his voice.

'Those chickens give you eggs?' said the other man. Willi
gave the men that morning's eggs.

The next morning he went back to St Martin's and told them
they could come take the furniture after all. A truck with two
different men came later that afternoon. Willi told them what to

take and what to leave. They carried it out into the garden. There it all stood, some of it elegant, all of it part of his story. But now it stood there, lost, without meaning or significance. The men loaded it into the truck and drove it away.

The long walks along the Isar or through the English Garden that Willi had loved before the war were not the same. There were homeless veterans everywhere, either manning barricades or shivering under makeshift shelters. And though the roses were blooming in the English Garden, the garish reds and yellows and their incessant bobbing in the breeze seemed to be mocking him. Their scent reminded him of death.

Crossing the footbridge over the Isar one September morning, Willi was overcome by a coughing fit – this still happened from time to time. He grabbed the iron railing and held on until the coughing subsided. Out of breath, his chest heaving, his throat raw, he looked down into the swollen river, churning brown and foamy. He imagined Ophelia drifting by. He gave her Eva's face. Her hair drifted around her white face; her mouth was open. Her eyes were looking at him as her dress pulled her under. The image was vivid and terrible, and Willi yearned to join her.

He could get over the railing, be in the water with one leap, and in another minute his pain would be over. But even before he could finish the thought, he knew he wouldn't do it. As soon as the icy water closed on him, he would be swimming for his life. And, he thought to himself, *who will take care of Puck?*

Willi felt dizzy. He closed his eyes and held on to the railing. It came down to a choice – didn't it? – between a hard life and the peace of the river. *Eternal freedom or the difficult here and now.* 'To be or not to be?' He laughed as he said the words aloud.

The outrageous fortune he had suffered in his still short life felt unbearable. And who knew what awfulness was yet to come? For now, though – right now – he could walk the fifteen minutes to Schillerstraße, cross the courtyard, through the door, past the desk sergeant, into the detectives' room, and sit down at the familiar wooden desk beside the mimeograph machine with the sign on it that said Detective W. Geismeier.

There – right there – a stack of documents connected with an insurance fraud case waited. The next hour would pass as he read through the files for information or leads. He would solve the case eventually; he was pretty sure of that. Or maybe he wouldn't. But there would always be another case. He would go home, make supper, feed Puck, go to bed. The next day would pass in a similar fashion, and the day after that, and the one after that. That was how it always worked: an entire lifetime would go by, moment by moment by moment.

Willi felt his despair breaking, like the spring ice. The river below him became just the Isar again, a river without implication. He let go of the railing, gathered himself, and continued across the bridge. He walked along Schillerstraße, stopped at the little bar for a cup of coffee. It tasted good; it tasted like the start of something. He crossed the street, went into the courtyard. The Italian florist recognized him and sang, '*Guten Morgen*,' hardening the *t* and rolling the *r* on his tongue so it sounded more Italian than German.

The Blau-Weiß Printing Company was in a large four-story warehouse in Ludwigstadt, not that far from Geismeier Ceramics. The building had been converted into offices and workshops before the war. A textile manufacturer, a book publisher, a distributor of medical supplies, an import-export company, and Blau-Weiß Printing had been there, but now most of those offices were abandoned and padlocked. A communist militia had taken over one end of the building. Of the earlier companies, only the import-export company and the printing company remained.

Neither Willi nor his badge impressed the communist guard who had stationed himself just inside the front door. He wore a red armband and a hat that he imagined made him look Russian. He sat with his feet on the table and slid his finger down a page. 'Your name's not on the list. You can't go up,' he said.

'I didn't ask for permission. I asked where their offices are,' said Willi.

The guard put an astonished look on his face. 'Don't you understand German, *Kamerad*?' he said. He took his feet off the table and stood up, as though he meant to stop Willi from going any further. This was how things were now; in a society coming apart, everybody thinks they're in charge.

'Whatever you're thinking of doing,' said Willi, 'think again.'

The guard, not a big or courageous or astute man, looked at Willi. Willi didn't look like much. Young, tall, thin, glasses, holding a badge toward him. But for reasons he didn't himself understand, the guard said, 'Fourth floor.'

Willi climbed to the fourth floor. At the top of the stairs was a heavy steel door with a sign that said Blau-Weiß Printing. Willi opened the door and was met by the rhythmic racket of a printing operation and the pungent smell of printers' ink. Spring sunlight slanted in through the tall windows. Willi asked a clerk to direct him to the person in charge. The clerk pointed to an enclosed cubicle. A man in a printer's apron stood behind a man sitting at a desk peering through a loupe. Willi knocked on the door and went in.

'Yes?' said the man without looking up.

Willi held up his badge. 'I'm from the police, Detective Geismeier,' he said. 'This post-office box is rented in your company's name.' The man looked up and Willi gave him a slip of paper with the box number on it.

'What's this about?' said the man.

'Is this your post-office box?' said Willi.

The man looked at Willi.

Willi looked back. The man sighed, got up, went to the door, and waved for one of the clerks to come in. 'Is this our PO box?' he said, handing him the paper.

The clerk found a ledger, opened it and slid his finger down the page. 'Yes, it is,' he said. 'But I thought we'd got rid of it.'

'We got rid of it?' said the boss to the clerk. 'Well, who was supposed to get rid of it?'

'Gabek,' said the clerk, checking the ledger. 'Gabek was supposed to close it out.'

'Get Gabek in here,' said the boss.

Gabek claimed at first that he had canceled the box. There must be some mistake. But he soon wrapped himself in a web of lies, and finally confessed that he hadn't canceled the box. Someone had offered him money to let them use the box for unknown purposes.

Willi stood with Gabek while he cleared out his locker. Gabek swore he didn't know the person, didn't know who he was, had never even seen him. He said he had answered a classified ad in the paper. 'AGENT NEEDED. Payment for service rendered,' followed by a classified ad box number.

Gabek said he didn't even know what the box was used for, had never seen the insurance forms. When Willi showed him one, Gabek looked away. 'Read it,' said Willi.

Gabek studied the form. 'Out loud,' said Willi. Gabek tried to sound out a few words. He couldn't read.

'How'd you read the classified ad?' said Willi.

'A friend read it to me. From the *Kurier.*'

Willi followed up with the newspaper, but they didn't find the ad. Gabek was charged and convicted of fraud which the prosecutor called noxious and disgusting – running an insurance swindle and stealing money from the fearful and the grieving. Gabek swore up and down he had nothing to do with the swindle, but the judge said that didn't matter. He had been a participant, knowing or unknowing. He agreed with the prosecutor that the swindle was evil and gave Gabek three years in Stadelheim Prison. Gabek wailed that his life was over. 'You should have thought of that before you got involved in crime,' said the judge, and Gabek was led off in shackles.

TWO CASES

L udwig came to Willi with a case. 'A drug case,' he said. 'Trouble is, I'm not sure it's even a case.'

'Is that case still alive?' said Ove. 'You really think there's something there, Ludwig?'

'Drugs are still going missing, Ove,' said Ludwig.

'Various drugs, small quantities,' he said, turning to Willi. 'Such small quantities, I mean, that nobody noticed for a long time.' Finally someone had seen discrepancies in the narcotics registry at the Ludwig Maximilian University hospital dispensary. Was it a crime or just an error? Nobody could say. 'I started to tell you about this before you got sick,' said Ludwig. 'You don't remember. Anyway, once they noticed the discrepancy, they started tracking other drugs, and the same sort of discrepancies showed up. And these weren't even narcotics. The hospital dispensary sent inquiries to other hospitals, clinics, pharmacies. And six different places reported they had drugs going missing too – always in small quantities. But the small quantities add up over time to big quantities.'

Ludwig gave Willi a list. 'Morphine, amphetamine, but mostly stuff you've never heard of. I've got a chemist working on it. Trying to figure out what the drugs have in common, if anything; how they might be used, since some of them don't have any uses besides medical.'

'How long has it been going on?' said Willi.

'Six months we know about, but probably longer.'

'Is it just drugs or is there anything else going missing?' said Willi.

'All we know about are the drugs,' said Ludwig.

'Is there some connection between all the different instances?' said Willi.

'I think so. It seems like too many to be coincidental. But to be honest, after all this time, I'm just guessing.'

'Then why is this even a case?' said Willi.

'Because it's drugs,' said Ove.

'Are people being poisoned or are these drugs somehow finding their way to the street?' said Willi.

'Neither one, as far as we know,' said Ludwig.

'But would we be able to tell?' said Willi.

'It's medical stuff, which means it's very pure. I think we'd know by now.'

'Maybe it's not about narcotics; maybe it's about the boring drugs, the ones no one pays attention to,' said Willi.

Ludwig thought about that for a moment. He laid a fat folder in front of Willi. 'Here's what I've got so far, Willi. Look it over. See if I'm missing something.'

'All right,' said Ove. 'You see, Geismeier? You've got some catching up to do.'

'Yes, Sergeant,' said Willi.

At his desk, Willi leafed back and forth through the file, comparing facts and making notations in his little notepad as he went along. After a while he left the room and came back from the book room carrying a thick pharmaceutical encyclopedia.

Then he went looking for a chemistry book. By the end of the day, his desk, which had been bare that morning, was covered with layers of open volumes and files.

Willi was still at it hours later, when Ludwig knocked on the sergeant's door and went in. 'What is it?' said Ove.

'That kid is going to kill himself, Ove,' said Ludwig.

Ove looked puzzled.

'Geismeier,' said Ludwig. 'He's working nonstop . . .'

Ove nodded.

'. . . and he looks like death warmed over,' said Ludwig.

'He does look rough around the edges,' said Ove, 'that's for sure. You worried about him?'

'A little,' said Ludwig. 'He's a good kid, and he's been through hell – the war, then the girlfriend, then his parents. Christ of mercy! He needs a break. He needs to give *himself* a break.'

'You know? I think that's what he's doing,' said Ove.

'What do you mean?'

'He's giving himself a break. From his life. Look, Ludwig, the one thing he loves right now is work. And it's the one thing that loves him back. Well, besides that cat. Anyway, investigating, finding clues, putting things together, that's his bread and butter. That's what makes him tick. And he's damn good at it. I mean . . . like that question "what if it's about the boring drugs?" Where did that come from? You didn't think of that; neither did I. He's good at this. It's his refuge. I think he's doing exactly what he needs to do to save himself.'

That night Willi dug out his old case notes from before the war. He marveled at his handwriting then – it was like a schoolboy's. He had been very thorough; everything was there. Eventually he found his interview with the old Count Wittelsbach. Procurement corruption for hospitals. Drugs had been involved. He found the articles Helmutt Arenz had written. He wrote down the names of the hospital board members and other names that had come up too. Just so he would have them at hand if they came up again.

The next morning Willi brought more books with him. He studied through the morning.

'Come on, Willi,' said Ludwig as the Frauenkirche was ringing one thirty. 'Let's go. I'll buy you lunch.'

Willi looked around, startled.

'They stop serving soon,' said Ludwig. 'Come on.'

The worker canteen nearby had bean soup, a sausage and roll, and a liter of beer, for two marks. The place was still pretty full. Even though the air in Munich was thick with revolt and upheaval these days, there were no disputes here, no name calling, just men coming and going and eating. Somehow politics seemed to stop at the door when a cheap lunch was involved.

When they had first met months earlier, Ludwig, astonished by Willi's youth, had remarked that he had grandchildren older than Willi. He was old enough for it to be true, but he had neither children nor grandchildren. And so he had now taken this suffering young man into his heart. He wanted to do something for him.

They ate in silence, Willi thinking about chemistry and medicine and corruption and the terrible *Spanische Grippe*, and Ludwig watching him eat and wondering how he could help. Finally he said, 'You learning anything, Geismeier?'

'About the case?' said Willi.

Ludwig nodded. 'Sure.'

Willi said he was learning about some of the drugs and chemicals that had gone missing. There were the narcotics, of course. But others, when mixed together or acted upon by other chemicals or by chemical processes, could be used to manufacture everything you could imagine. 'For instance, creosote is one of the drugs that has gone missing from several locations, even though it is not a controlled substance. You can buy it as *Aqua creosoti* at most pharmacies. In small doses it's used as an anesthetic or a sedative. Some doctors are even prescribing a creosote compound to treat the *Grippe*. Sometimes it's also combined with eucalyptus oil. So I have to ask, if it's so easily available, why is it being stolen?'

'And what's the answer?' said Ludwig.

'I don't have one,' said Willi.

'Do the drugs have other uses you haven't mentioned?'

'They're also used in medical testing,' said Willi.

'No ideas then?' said Ludwig.

Willi shrugged and smiled. 'No ideas. Not yet. Sorry. What about you, Ludwig? You've been on this case longer than me.'

'What did you mean when you asked about the boring drugs yesterday, the non-narcotics?'

'It was just a question, that's all. I mean, even aspirin might have sinister uses.'

'And that's what you're looking into? With all the books, I mean?'

'Sort of,' said Willi. 'Mainly I'm just looking for ideas right now. Trying to stir things up in my brain.' He smiled again.

They had finished eating. They carried their dishes to the dishwashing counter and then left to walk back to the office.

'Are you going to be all right, Willi?' said Ludwig.

'Thanks, Ludwig,' said Willi. 'I'll be fine. I promise.'

Ove Sandheim called a precinct meeting to explain the new order of things. 'Effective immediately,' he said, 'we're no longer under the control of the army. All police are now under civilian control. It remains to be seen *which* civilians – Munich, Bavaria, or the new German republic. For now it's the republic, but . . .'

The men looked at one another and groaned. 'I shit on the republic,' said one, and a couple of others muttered their agreement.

'All right: that's enough of that!' said Ove. He stood up and planted his huge fists on his hips. 'I don't give a shit whether you favor communists, socialists, or Hottentots,' he said. 'Just don't bring your political shit to work with you. You do, and I'll have your ass out of here so fast it will make your head spin. Is that clear?'

'Yes, Sergeant,' said some. Others muttered again.

Ove took a step toward the mutterers. 'What was that?' he said.

'Yes, Sergeant,' they said.

'All right then,' he said.

Ove knew he was shouting into the wind. What he called political shit would find its way into police business, no matter what. The communists and fascists were dividing up the city, fighting over territory, fighting over control, and the fascists were winning the battle.

Ove dismissed the patrolmen from the meeting. The four detectives – Willi and his partner Ludwig Voss, and Karl

Redelmann and Moritz Busch – stayed behind. Karl and Moritz had just started working on a murder, their first case since their transfer from another precinct. The body of a police informer – a minor gangster – had just been fished out of a cesspool behind an ironworks. He had been tortured and then executed with a single bullet behind the ear. 'Plenty of people wanted him dead,' said Moritz, 'and plenty were willing to do the job. We're running down suspects. Their names are up on the board.' Everybody turned to look. 'If you guys can think of other names that should be up there, let us know.'

'OK,' said Ove. 'Any more on that? No? Then what about the insurance fraud? Where is that?'

'Ladislaw Gabek's in prison,' said Willi. 'We have the post-office box under surveillance and we're collecting the contents as they come in, which is still happening. But nobody is showing up to collect it. So somehow they know we're on to them.'

'Nobody? So, do you think it was Gabek after all?' said Ove.

'I think so,' said Willi. 'But not alone. He's not up to it. Folks are still applying for coverage, although not as many as before.'

'Anything interesting there?' said Ove.

'The application forms are interesting,' said Willi.

'What do you mean?' said Ove.

'Well, there are more questions than you usually find on these forms. The usual stuff about your medical conditions, prescription drugs. But questions about your parents, your mother's maiden name, blood type, complexion, racial and ethnic stuff.'

'What do you make of that?' said Ludwig.

'I don't know,' said Willi. 'It struck me as odd. It's something to keep in mind. And more claims are coming in, too. But there's something else: other stuff coming in.'

'What other stuff?' said Ove.

'Well, some catalogues for medical supplies.'

'What kind of medical supplies?' said Ludwig.

'Some equipment, some pharmaceuticals. From different companies.'

'Is that interesting?' said Ove.

'Maybe,' said Willi. 'There were also some invoices.'

'Invoices – for what?' said Ove.

'There are different invoices from Rosenberg Medical Supplies for some replacement parts for a centrifuge and a precision scale.'

'Sent to?'

'A Herr Basiky, vice president.'

'Vice president of what?'

'It doesn't say.'

'Why is that interesting?' said Ove.

'Yeah,' said Ludwig. 'Catalogues and invoices could end up in that box by mistake.'

'Maybe,' said Willi.

'But that's not what you're thinking, is it?' said Ove.

'A scale like the one on the invoice – someone ordered it and failed to pay – is mostly used in laboratories for taking precise measurements of chemicals. And a centrifuge is used to separate out chemical components.'

'Wait a minute,' said Ludwig, 'are you talking about the fraud case or the drug case?'

'I don't know,' said Willi. 'Maybe both.'

PRISONER 61757

Nothing about the two cases seemed the same: an insurance scam and missing drugs. But they intersected in the post-office box, which was odd. Willi thought the intersection was worth at least looking into.

'I guess so; you never know, unless you look,' said Ludwig, sounding doubtful.

'I think you're wasting your time, Geismeier,' said Ove. 'You're imagining connections that don't exist.'

'You mean like Birnam Wood coming to Dunsinane?' said Willi. 'Never mind,' he said, seeing the baffled look on their faces. Nobody ever got his Shakespeare allusions. 'Give me half a day, Sergeant. A quick interview with Gabek and a conversation with Rosenberg Medical, and we'll know if there's a connection or not.'

'All right,' said Ove. 'You've got tomorrow morning. Then get back to following up with the insurance claims.'

The Stadelheim Prison was of a classical design. At first glance it suggested an institution of higher learning more than a prison. And this morning the sun cast it in a rosy light. Recently planted plane trees lined the entire front of the building, and their large leaves shivered in the morning breeze. Once you passed through the trees, though, and approached the visitors' entry, the watchtowers came into view. Then you noticed the windows were small and barred.

The door was heavy dark wood crisscrossed with metal straps. Inside, the walls and ceilings were gray granite. Lamps were bare bulbs in metal cages. The yellow brick floors gleamed. They had been washed down that morning, as they were every morning. There were drains every five meters. A heavy iron grate reached wall to wall and floor to ceiling across a corridor that all but disappeared into the distant gloom. Two guards waited at a desk by the gate.

One guard checked the logbook to see that Willi was expected. He took Willi's identification card and badge. The other guard stepped forward, signaled to Willi that he should raise his arms and spread his legs. He patted him down. The one sitting at the desk lifted the receiver from the phone, waited for a response at the other end, and said, 'Geismeier, Willi.' A voice from the phone said something Willi could not make out. '*Jawohl*,' said the guard and hung up the receiver.

Willi heard footsteps echoing along the corridor. A guard emerged from a side corridor and turned toward them. The standing guard took a ring of large keys from the desk and opened the gate. He signaled for Willi to step through, then closed the gate behind him with a clang.

'This way,' said the guard who had come to fetch him. They walked side by side down the long corridor. It was devoid of decoration or furnishings or even doors. A few windows high on the outside wall did little to brighten the place. They turned down another corridor, this one lined with doors on both sides. The guard unlocked a door and they went into a narrow room with a high vaulted ceiling. High in an alcove on one wall was a window, and higher still – for some reason – was a wooden crucifix. Maybe this had once been a chapel.

There was a massive wooden table with two facing heavy wooden chairs in the center of the room, all bolted to the floor. A guard stood behind the chair on which Gabek sat, so utterly still and thoroughly diminished that Willi didn't notice him at first. He looked like a shriveled child trying his best to avoid being seen. He was disheveled, badly shaved, with red-rimmed eyes that followed Willi as he walked to the chair opposite him and sat down.

Gabek's prison shirt was badly worn and much too large. The collar was frayed, the sleeves too. A patch stitched to his right chest said 61757. 'Hello, Herr Gabek,' said Willi.

Gabek didn't answer.

'Hello, Herr Gabek,' said Willi again.

'I don't feel well,' said Gabek.

'Are you ill?' said Willi.

The guard stepped closer to Gabek.

Gabek flinched and didn't say anything.

'If you're ill, Herr Gabek, there is a prison infirmary,' said Willi.

'I'm all right,' said Gabek.

'I have a few questions for you,' said Willi. 'Do you feel well enough to answer my questions?'

Gabek didn't say anything. He closed his eyes for a long instant, as though he were bracing himself for an unpleasant procedure.

'First of all, Herr Gabek, let me say I believe you when you say you don't know who was using the post-office box.'

A look of relief crossed Gabek's face and then just as quickly disappeared.

'Once you had arranged for them to use it, were you ever in communication with them?'

'No. Never,' said Gabek.

'Weren't you curious to know who they were, Herr Gabek?'

'No, never,' said Gabek.

'So, when you were picking up mail from the other Blau-Weiß mailboxes, you never encountered that person?'

'No, never.'

'And you never tried to discover who they might be?'

'I told you all this before,' said Gabek.

'I know you did,' said Willi. 'Did you ever have occasion to collect the contents of the post-office box? Or if not, did you ever see what was in the box?'

'No,' said Gabek. 'I never collected it.'

'And did you ever see what was in it?'

'No. I told you, I never saw any of that.'

The phrase struck Willi as odd. It made him think Gabek might have seen the forms and payments. 'What do you mean by "any of that?"' said Willi.

Gabek corrected himself. 'I never saw anything that was in the box,' he said. 'I just let them use the box. Like I said. That was all I did. I just let them use the box.'

'Herr Gabek,' said Willi, 'were you aware of medical supplies coming or going through that post-office box, either drugs or other things?'

'No, I never saw anything,' said Gabek. The guard behind Gabek's chair had put his hand on the back of the chair and had now stepped forward, apparently to remind him of his presence.

Gabek kept his eyes locked on Willi's. The guard standing over him was in uniform, but unlike the other guards, he was not wearing a name tag or a badge. He was medium height, maybe three inches shorter than Willi, with a thick neck and sloping shoulders. He had thick lips, and a small mustache that had been dyed brown. He had narrow, unblinking gray eyes. Willi looked for other identifying marks but saw none. He tried to make a mental note of the man's face, but it was not the kind of thing Willi was good at.

'So you were never there when the contents were collected?' said Willi. 'You were never there when that doctor came to collect the mail?'

'No,' said Gabek. 'How many times do I have to tell you?'

The guard's eyes narrowed slightly. 'Are you finished, Detective?' he said.

'Yes, I'm finished,' said Willi. 'Thank you.' He stood up.

Without a moment's hesitation, the guard who had brought Willi to the room stepped forward from the door where he had been waiting. Gabek remained seated with his guard still standing behind him. That guard now had a hand on Gabek's shoulder. They waited while Willi was escorted from the room.

Back at the gate, Willi collected his badge and identification and left the building. The plane trees with their leaves shimmering green and silver in the sun were a welcome sight.

POOR GABEK

Until recently Rosenberg Medical Supplies had been a small family business barely providing a living for the four Rosenbergs – the parents and two grown children. But since the *Spanische Grippe* outbreak, their fortunes had changed. Their products were in great demand now, and Rosenberg Medical Supplies had grown into a substantial operation, hiring clerks and delivery people as needed until they now numbered twenty-five. Heinrich Rosenberg, the president and son of the founder, was proud of their success. He gave Willi a company brochure and a catalogue. You never knew who might be a future customer. He insisted on showing Willi around the new offices, which, he said, they had already outgrown.

Every available space had boxes stacked to the ceiling. Six people worked at a long table studying invoices, finding the required material from the shelves behind them, and packing it into boxes for delivery. Workers with hand trucks moved boxes out the door and on to trucks.

'This is Klaus,' said Rosenberg. 'He can answer all your questions.'

Willi gave Klaus the invoice for the centrifuge parts and the scale. 'I'm trying to learn what I can about this order,' said Willi.

Klaus studied the invoice, then went to a file drawer, where he rifled through the row of folders until he found one labeled Basiky. 'This order was fulfilled . . . last July. This is the third invoice we sent.'

'All to this box number?' said Willi.

'Yes.'

'And you're sure that was the correct box number?' said Willi.
Klaus took the order form from the file and handed it to
Willi. 'Basiky filled it out himself,' he said.

'Had he ever ordered from you before?'

'Never,' said Klaus. 'If he had, it would be in this file.'

'And was the order delivered to the PO box also?' said Willi.

'No, of course not. You can see right here. It was picked up.'

'So someone came here and got it. Is there some record
of that?'

'This signature here.' Klaus pointed to an illegible scribble at
the bottom of the invoice. 'That's the guy that picked it up.'

'And is that the guy that ordered it?'

'No way of knowing,' said Klaus.

'And what do you know about him?' said Willi.

'Other than that he's a deadbeat?' said Klaus. 'Nothing.'

'Might he have been a doctor or other medical person?'

'I don't know,' said Klaus. 'I suppose he might have been. But
he might not have been. I don't know.'

Before he left, Willi wanted to speak to Heinrich Rosenberg
again. He showed him the invoice. 'Is this the kind of equipment
people regularly order from you?'

'Yes,' said Heinrich.

'And who usually orders such things?'

'Small clinics, small laboratories, small pharmacies, mostly.'

'Not big hospitals or pharmaceutical companies?' said Willi.

'A big hospital or lab would order these scales by the dozen.
And these centrifuges rarely get repaired. The big labs throw
them out. In fact, it's rare for anyone to repair these things.
This is an old model. I'd expect when it broke down, you'd
just replace it.'

'So what would prompt someone to want to repair it instead
of replacing it?'

'I can't think of any reason,' said Heinrich. 'Unless they're just
trying to save money. Or they don't want someone to know they
have a centrifuge.'

'And why wouldn't you want it known you have a centrifuge?'

Heinrich gave it some thought. 'Well, basically you're separating things into their components or extracting elements. So
you might be doing secret research you don't want anyone to

know about. A new medicine maybe, a secret cure for the *Grippe* or something like that. Or you could be extracting drugs that you would then be remixing for illicit purposes, making illegal drugs, inventing new narcotics. Is that what you think is happening, Herr Detective?'

Willi didn't answer. He didn't know what was happening. He didn't know whether he had found something or nothing. Yes, Gabek was being intimidated by a prison guard. And Gabek hadn't contradicted Willi when he said a doctor had picked up the mail. That could be something. Someone was repairing a centrifuge and not paying his bills. But what did that add up to? Nothing. Meanwhile, the insurance fraudsters were still as unknown to him as they had been when he had first learned of their fraud.

Ove and Ludwig listened to Willi's report in silence. Willi sat looking at his hands, which he folded and unfolded on the desk in front of him. Then Ove said, 'Let's forget the drugs for now; let's focus on the fraud. Look at known insurance fraudsters, where they are now, what they're doing. Get back to the basics.'

'And yet,' said Willi, 'I think something bigger is going on, and Gabek may be the key. He's terrified, and someone is making sure he doesn't say anything, which tells me he's a witness to something bigger than either insurance fraud or drugs.'

Ove thought about that for a moment.

'I want to visit Gabek again,' said Willi.

'Why?' said Ludwig.

Willi didn't have a good answer. The trouble was there were no 'where-were-you-on-the-night-of' questions, no 'do-you-know-so-and-so' questions. Gabek was a man alone. He might not even know what he knew. And there was something to Willi's thesis that Gabek's terror was out of all proportion to the so-called crimes they were investigating. 'OK,' said Ove. 'Talk to him, and keep us posted.'

Willi went to Stadelheim early the next morning. His identification and badge were collected. He heard the footsteps echoing down the hall before he saw the guard round the corner and approach the gate. Then the three guards had a whispered conversation, and the guard who had come down the hall went back the way he had come.

The two guards at the gate signaled for Willi to approach. The one seated at the desk handed Willi's badge and identification back to him, 'Prisoner 61757 is unavailable today.'

'Unavailable?' said Willi.

'He's ill,' said the second guard.

'How ill?' said Willi.

The guard just shook his head.

THE WARDEN

The prison warden refused to give Willi any information about Gabek's condition, when and how he had fallen ill, or even who the attending physician was. And by the time Willi could return with a warrant compelling the warden to share what he knew, Gabek was dead.

'Are you related to the prisoner?' said the warden.

'No,' said Willi. 'I didn't know him, except as a witness.'

'And yet you want to see the body?'

'Yes,' said Willi.

'Epidemic protocol prohibits it. And doctor's orders,' said the warden. He held up the death certificate. Willi asked to see it and the warden handed it to him. The cause of death was listed as *Spanische Grippe*.

'He is to be buried immediately,' said the warden.

'Where?' said Willi.

'It must be done quickly so it will be here' – the warden pointed back behind him with his thumb – 'in the prison graveyard.'

'Does Stadelheim have physicians on staff?' said Willi.

'We have a rotating group of physicians from the university hospital,' said the warden.

'Who attended him, and who declared him dead?' said Willi. The signature on the death certificate was illegible.

'We aren't allowed to give out names,' said the warden. 'For the doctors' protection. You'll have to ask at the university hospital.'

'Did Gabek leave behind any personal effects?' said Willi.

'Nothing much. A watch, writing materials – pen, ink, some writing paper, as well as a couple of books, a Bible, that's about it.'

Willi thought about that for a moment. 'Did he have any family?'

'His next of kin is listed as a sister,' said the warden.

'Will you be notifying his sister that he has died?' he said.

'That's what the prison chaplain is for,' said the warden.

'Unless I am able to look at the body, I'm going to report this as a suspicious death.'

'Why is that?' said the warden.

'He was a witness in an ongoing criminal investigation. When I spoke with him recently, he was frightened but apparently healthy. The guard accompanying him was clearly intimidating him. Now he's dead. At the time of death on the death certificate, the guards were telling me he was ill, not that he was dead.

'In addition to seeing the body, I want to interview those guards as well as the guard that was with Gabek when I first interviewed him.'

'You'll need warrants,' said the warden.

Once again, Willi found himself walking down a long gray granite corridor with a yellow tile floor, this time with the warden on his left and the prison coroner on his right. The morgue was in a narrow, low-ceiling, brightly lit room. There were several metal tables on wheels lined up end to end along one wall and a double row of square metal lockers set into the opposite wall. Through the window high on the wall at the far end of the room, above the porcelain sink and counter, Willi saw the leaves of the plane trees out on the street. The wind had stopped and the leaves just hung there. In the morgue, the strong smell of formaldehyde almost masked the stench of decay. The warden rarely visited the morgue. He had taken out his handkerchief and covered his nose.

The coroner checked his list, opened one of the lockers and pulled out a steel drawer with a body wrapped in a shroud lying in it. He pulled back the shroud revealing the thin, naked, gray corpse of Gabek, his mouth pressed closed, his arms folded across his midsection. There were no serious injuries showing on the body, but above his right wrist there was bruising and a constellation of black spots where injections had apparently been administered.

'You'll have to ask his doctor about that,' said the warden.

Willi saw the guards one by one – the two from the front gate and the one who walked him back to see Gabek. He asked them about Gabek's illness and his treatment, but they didn't know anything. They all said the same thing. 'He was treated in the infirmary.'

Willi asked the guard who had walked him back and forth about the guard that had been with Gabek. 'I didn't know him,' said the guard.

'Do you know his name?' said Willi.

'I don't know anything about him,' said the guard.

'Had you seen him before?'

'Not that I remember,' said the guard.

'So you don't know the other guards in Stadelheim?' said Willi.

'Some of them, but not all of them,' said the guard.

'Anything else?' said the warden.

'I need to see that guard, the one that was there with Gabek,' said Willi.

The warden studied the logbook for what seemed to Willi to be a long time. When the guard finally appeared, he had a name tag and badge number – Ammer, 1256 – but it was not the same man. This man was taller, heavier, and didn't have a mustache. He had a tattoo showing above his collar.

Willi and the man looked at one another. 'Herr Ammer,' said Willi, 'how long have you been a guard here at Stadelheim?'

'Four years,' said the guard. The warden shifted uneasily from one foot to the other.

'Have you ever met me before?'

'Once, the day you visited the prisoner Gabek,' said Ammer.

'Do you remember what day and time that was, Herr Ammer?'

Ammer named the day and time.

'Do you remember whether the prisoner was ill or not?'

'Yes, he was quite ill,' said Ammer. 'He was feverish and was having trouble breathing.'

Willi turned to the warden. 'Warden, how many guards do you have in Stadelheim?'

The warden was startled to be questioned. 'What is this about, Detective?' he said.

'Do you know all the guards in your prison personally? Would you be able to recognize them by sight?'

'Listen, Detective . . .'

'Warden, this man is not the man who was watching over prisoner 61757, Ladislaw Gabek, when I visited.'

'Is this true, Ammer?' said the warden, turning toward the guard. Willi could see the warden check the man's name tag.

'No, sir, Herr Warden,' said the guard. 'The Herr Detective is mistaken. I remember the detective quite well. I was there through the entire interrogation.'

'Warden,' said Willi, 'when I interviewed the prisoner, the guard with him had no badge or name tag. He had a dyed mustache and no tattoo on his neck.'

Ammer raised his hand to his neck. A part of the index finger on his right hand was missing. 'You're wrong about that, Detective. I was there.'

'Where are you working today, Ammer?' said the warden, checking his logbook.

'Section C, Block 8, Herr Warden,' said Ammer, snapping to attention.

'All right, Ammer,' said the warden, 'return to your post.' Ammer saluted and left the room.

The warden waited until Ammer was out of the room before he spoke. 'Detective Geismeier, I run a tight ship here. I don't like it, don't like it *at all*, a junior cop coming in here and making all sorts of wild accusations. Either you are misremembering, or you are playing some sort of game with me, and either way I don't like it. I don't know what you think you're doing, but I have a prison to run. Your chief will be hearing from me.' The warden walked Willi to the gate and had one of the guards there escort him all the way out of the building.

Back in his office, the warden looked at the board with today's assignments. There it was written in chalk – Section C, Block 8 – *Ammer/Bäder*. 'I knew it,' said the warden and sat down at his desk to find his way back into the morning's business. 'A damned waste of time!' he said. 'Unbelievable!'

After a few minutes though, for whatever reason, the warden felt uneasy. That Geismeier had seemed very sure of himself. What if he was on to something going on right under the warden's nose? No, that couldn't be. He knew his prison and he knew his men. Actually, he didn't know Ammer that well at all. He knew the name, and the man had looked familiar to him, or at least he thought so.

After standing up and sitting back down again a few times, the warden finally decided he should go have a word with Ammer, hear his side of things again, and lay the whole damn unpleasant thing to rest for good.

The guards at the gate let him in, and one walked with him as prison regulations required. Section C, Block 8 was at the furthest end of the prison. It was where the psych cases were housed. Someone was always shouting or crying there. It was the warden's least favorite part of his institution, even worse than the morgue.

And, sure enough, as they approached the guard station at C-8, someone was screaming and cursing and hurling themselves against the door of one of the cells. 'I am Jesus Christ, I am Satan! Believe in me!' screamed the man, over and over.

One of the guards was on his way to put a stop to the ruckus. The other guard sat at the station, his jacket off, his chair tipped back. He was reading a magazine. This kind of hubbub went on all the time and he was used to it. So he was oblivious to the approaching warden.

When he finally saw the warden, it was too late. He nearly tipped over on the chair and dropped the magazine, trying to jump into his jacket and salute at the same time. 'Herr Warden!' he shouted. He was a man of fifty or so, balding, a white Kaiser mustache, reading glasses on his nose, short, bow-legged with a pot belly.

'Never mind, Bäder, it's all right,' said the warden. 'I'm here to talk to Herr Ammer. I'll wait until he's finished over there.' The noise had already stopped. 'He'll be right back. No problem. I'll wait.'

'But, Herr Warden,' said the guard, standing at attention and holding his salute, '*I'm Ammer. That's Bäder over there.* Apologies, Herr Warden. But I am Ammer.'

ROUNDS

The university hospital had something of Stadelheim about it. There was a long corridor whose floor was made of those same yellow bricks. The hospital corridor had office doors along one side and patients waited on wooden chairs and benches along the opposite wall. Electric lamps had recently been hung from the ceiling replacing gas lamps, but they still glowed too dimly to dispel the gloom.

Occasionally a door would open, a man in a white coat would come out of an office and call a name. A patient would follow him into the office, and the door would close. Those still waiting would crane their necks, trying for a glimpse inside. When a patient visit was finished, they left by a different door that led into another corridor, so to those waiting it looked as if people went in and never came out.

At the end of the hall was a wooden door with a bronze plaque that read 'The Ludwig Maximilian Hospital, Professor Doctor Wilhelm August Schäuble, General Director.' Willi knocked on the door, waited a moment, and went in. He told the receptionist inside that he had an appointment to speak with Director Schäuble. 'Detective Willi Geismeier,' he said.

She gave Willi a doubtful look, but on examining her appointment book and finding his name, she said he should have a seat and she would see if Professor Doctor Schäuble would see him. She reappeared after several minutes. 'The Herr Professor Doctor is very busy today and asks that you complete your business expeditiously.'

The Herr professor doctor – protocol required that all his titles be used – sat behind a huge desk, working his way through a stack of papers in front of him, signing the top one, laying it aside, then reading and signing the next. He signed three or four more pages, glanced up at Willi for a moment, then went back to signing and turning pages. 'Yes?' he said without looking up again.

'Herr Doctor,' Willi said, taking a small notebook from his pocket, 'a prisoner named Gabek has just died at Stadelheim Prison. I believe the attending physician is a member of your hospital staff. I would like to talk with him about the prisoner's death.'

'Why do you need to talk to him?' said Schäuble, laying the pen aside and looking Willi up and down for the first time. His face revealed that he did not like what he saw.

'It has to do with a criminal investigation, Herr Doctor, so if you would just give me his name . . .'

'I most certainly will not give you anyone's name without knowing the reason.'

Willi held up his badge for Schäuble to see. 'Detective Willi Geismeier,' he said in case the doctor had not heard him the first time. 'And I need the name of the doctor who last attended the deceased prisoner.'

'Young man!' said Schäuble, 'I have no intention of giving you the doctor's name.'

'Herr Schäuble, I can get a court order, if you require it. But trying to keep me from speaking with this doctor would waste your time and mine . . .'

The doctor snorted and shook his head in exasperation at the suggestion that his priorities and those of this young, rude policeman could in any way be regarded as equal. Nevertheless, he pushed the button on his intercom.

'*Jawohl*, Herr Professor Doctor?' came the receptionist's voice.

'Frau Becker, where is Herr Doctor von Fischer at this hour?' Frau Becker did not know exactly, but she said she would find out. 'Would you please give that information to the young detective who is now leaving? Thank you.

'Now, detective, if there's nothing else . . .'

'As a matter of fact, there is,' said Willi. 'There is the matter of drugs going missing from your hospital. I have learned that, after doing an internal investigation, you decided not to notify the police about these missing drugs. Could you tell me, please, Herr Doctor, how you reached that decision?'

'As I already told your chief, Detective, we conducted a thorough investigation and concluded that the theft of these drugs is of no concern to the police. Now, if you will . . .'

'But how did you determine that the police should not be brought in?'

'I must insist, young—'

'Was it you, Doctor, who decided not to notify the police, or someone else?'

'My staff and I, we met and discussed—'

'I would like a list of everyone who was involved in that decision.'

'Why on earth would you need such a list? I've told you, young man, we have decided—'

Willi opened the little notebook again. 'I'm ready when you are, Doctor,' he said.

The director rolled his eyes. Willi asked who had led the investigation, how had the investigation been conducted – were multiple people interviewed, which people. Did the director have any thoughts as to why the drugs had been taken, how they had been taken? 'Do you know who took them?'

'Of course,' said Schäuble. 'The thief is a disgruntled former employee, a laboratory technician. He has disappeared.'

'His name?' said Willi.

'It's in the report.' He pushed the intercom button again. 'Frau Becker, give the detective our report on the missing drugs as well. He's just leaving.'

'One more thing, Herr Doctor. Has any other medical equipment gone missing that you haven't reported?'

'What do you have in mind, Detective?' said Schäuble.

'Anything: test tubes, flasks, microscopes? Anything.'

'See here, Detective, we don't keep track of that kind of thing. There's always breakage, things go missing, get misplaced. Test tubes get used and thrown out by the thousands.'

'Microscopes, scales, centrifuges?' said Willi.

'You need to talk to our laboratory director about that. Is that finally all?'

Willi folded his notebook and put it in his pocket. 'Thank you, Herr Schäuble,' he said and left the office. Frau Becker handed him the report. She said Herr Professor Doctor von Fischer was in Berlin for a conference. He would be back in his lab in the Theodor Drunz Building the following Monday.

Once Willi had left, Doctor Schäuble called Frau Becker into his office and dictated a letter to the Munich chief of detectives. He described the thoroughgoing rudeness and arrogance of a 'boy detective, named Geismeier.'

'This uneducated and ignorant fellow subjected me to a ridiculous interrogation about a case that was not by any stretch of imagination worth a minute of Munich's police department's time and resources.

'I and my staff, all highly educated and accomplished professionals, have looked into the facts and have concluded that a disgruntled employee stole the drugs in question. That employee was dismissed. He has now vanished and is therefore unavailable for questioning, although there is no doubt that he is the culprit. He is known to be uneducated, to have a drug habit, and to consort with what can most charitably be called marginal elements of society. That was all the evidence we needed. No further investigation is required.

'Moreover, Geismeier's lack of respect – not recognizing or respecting my authority in my own hospital – goes beyond the pale. I am sure you would agree with me that a person of Geismeier's immaturity and lack of respect for authority should never have been allowed to become a detective. He should be dismissed from the force, or at least reduced in rank to patrolman.'

On reading Schäuble's letter, the chief of detectives could not disagree that the detective's behavior at least sounded rude. At the same time, he also saw that Schäuble and his associates had been remiss by failing to file a police report. Still, he sent the letter across town to the chief of Geismeier's district with a handwritten note attached: 'Look into this, please.'

One morning Ove Sandheim found an official envelope on his desk with a note inside saying that the district chief wanted to see him on an important matter. A copy of Schäuble's letter was attached.

'See here, Sandheim,' said the chief as soon as Ove arrived in his office, 'what can you tell me about this detective' – he looked at the letter to see the name – 'Willi Geismeier?'

'First rate,' said Ove.

'Really? Well, he's certainly annoyed Professor Doctor Schäuble at the Ludwig Maximilian.'

'Yes, I read the letter.'

'That sort of behavior is unacceptable,' said the chief. 'Is Geismeier a Jew?'

'Chief,' said Ove, 'Detective Geismeier interviewed the head of the hospital where drugs went missing. The man felt insulted because Geismeier didn't use all his titles.'

'Well, you've got to show respect,' said the chief, feeling a little aggrieved himself.

'You're right, Chief,' said Ove. 'Geismeier's young and he'll learn.' Although Ove Sandheim, who was a good judge of character, was pretty sure that fawning or obeisance to authority was something Willi would never learn. 'But, Chief, consider this. In the few days since his interview with Schäuble – sorry, Herr Doctor Schäuble – Geismeier has opened a case that no one even knew was a case. He located the person the hospital chief singled out as the guilty party – he had by no means disappeared, as Doctor Schäuble said. The man, a lab assistant, had repeatedly been denied promotion because of a withered arm and now he was fired for something he didn't do.'

'Well,' said the chief, 'if he couldn't do the work as a cripple . . .'

'He did the work, Chief, but his supervisor said more than once, his handicap was off-putting to coworkers and patients. As for the so-called "marginal elements" he supposedly associates with, they turn out to run a soup kitchen. He's a volunteer there.'

'With a withered arm?' The chief made a sour face.

'Yes, Chief.'

'Are they Marxists?'

'Who?' said Ove.

'The soup kitchen people,' said the chief.

'I think they're from the Little Sisters of the Poor,' said Ove. The district chief gave Ove a long look. With Ove Sandheim you never knew when he was serious and when he was joking.

SOUP

Doctor Schäuble and his fellow 'investigators' had failed to find the missing lab tech, because they hadn't looked for him. 'As far as they're concerned, we're just part of the equipment,' another technician told Willi. 'Samuel Raschermann is a first-rate tech. And now, thanks to them, he's finished in the research field. You can probably find him at the Red Banner Kitchen in Schwabing.'

The soup kitchen was in a narrow dark room down an alley. A tattered red banner hung from a pole above the door. Two burly men stood guard at the entrance to the alley. Even though it was not yet nine in the morning, people – mostly women and children – were already lined up outside. They looked at Willi suspiciously as he walked past and went inside.

Maria Helig ran the place. She lived on a small inheritance, most of which she used to keep the Red Banner operation going. After Samuel was fired, she had given him a place to sleep in a vacant servant's room under the eaves in her building. She was always doing good; the kitchen workers called her Holy Mary. 'Heilige Maria instead of Maria Helig, get it?' It was the kind of joke a bunch of Catholic Marxists found amusing.

Maria was washing dishes in a large sink. The sleeves of her shirt were pulled up above her elbows. Her arms were red from the hours they spent in hot water. Her forehead and upper lip were wet with sweat, a strand of hair had slipped out of her bandana, and she brushed it out of her face with the back of a soapy hand. She directed Willi to Samuel cutting up vegetables.

Samuel braced the vegetables against his right forearm and peeled and chopped them with his left, as though peeling and chopping one handed was the most natural thing in the world.

Willi said he wanted to talk to Samuel about the missing drugs.

'It was me who reported them missing,' said Samuel. 'I didn't take them.'

'I know that,' said Willi.

'So what do you want from me?'

'I just have a few questions,' said Willi.

'Why?'

'Because you were there and you reported it,' said Willi.

'Would you rather go elsewhere to talk about it?'

Samuel looked Willi up and down. 'No, here is fine.' He kept peeling and chopping. 'Do you mind if I keep working?' Willi didn't mind. 'How'd you discover the drugs were missing?' he said.

'First, I noticed some narcotics weren't where they were supposed to be.'

'Where were they supposed to be?'

'In a locked cabinet. I had put them in and locked it when I logged them in.'

'And who had a key to the cabinet?'

'I did. And several doctors have keys, and I assume some of the assistants do too.'

'So the controls are pretty lax?'

'Very,' said Samuel. 'And I reported the lax controls too, more than once. To Gerhard Erzberger, the guy in charge. And to a couple of doctors.'

'To Schäuble, the director?' said Willi.

'No, not to him,' said Samuel. 'But I'm sure he knew.'

'Did they ever tighten up the controls?'

'Not that I could tell. The lock wasn't changed; the keys weren't collected.'

'Once the drugs went missing?'

'Not while I was still there; they hadn't done anything when I left.'

'Did you report the drugs missing right away?'

'As soon as I was sure they were missing.'

'Who'd you report it to?' said Willi.

'Erzberger,' said Samuel.

'The guy that had you fired,' said Willi.

'That's him,' said Samuel. 'Asshole. He's responsible for dispensing narcotics. At least two of the techs under him are addicted and selling.'

Samuel had finished peeling and chopping the potatoes, carrots, celery. He scooped them into a large steaming pot of lentils and greens.

'What did he say when you told him about the missing drugs?'

'Nothing. He just looked at me. I think he said he'd make a note of it, or something like that.'

'So, not concerned?'

'No.'

'Did you ever think you might have been fired because you reported the drugs missing?'

Samuel looked at Willi for a moment. 'No, Erzberger made it pretty clear why he was firing me.'

'Because he didn't want to look at you?'

'That's pretty much what he said,' said Samuel. 'Like I said: he's an asshole.'

'And why'd you report the drugs missing?' said Willi. 'Not everybody would have done that.'

'I thought at first it was somebody using or selling narcotics. I have a brother who's an addict. I know the damage drugs do.'

'But now you think it's not that, not somebody using?'

'No. I think it's something else.'

'Why do you think that?'

'Because it's not just narcotics.'

'I know about the other drugs,' said Willi. 'Are they taking equipment as well?'

'What equipment?' said Samuel.

'Anything – test tubes, microscopes?' said Willi.

'Test tubes, vials, that stuff is always disappearing. Other lab equipment? It comes and goes. Eventually something gets replaced and the old stuff gets carted off. So I wouldn't know what's being stolen.'

'And who decides when a piece is replaced?' said Willi.

'That would be Erzberger,' said Samuel.

'About the other drugs: couldn't they be taken to conceal the fact someone's taking the narcotics?'

'No,' said Samuel. 'The narcotics are locked up. The other stuff is unsecured and easy to steal. No, there's got to be more to it than getting high.'

'So, what do you think it is?' said Willi.

'I'm thinking it's someone experimenting with chemicals, making new chemical compounds.'

'What do you mean?' said Willi.

'Do you know anything about compounding chemicals?'

'No.'

'Well, if you ask me, that's what's going on. Somebody is breaking down drugs and combining their elements in new ways.'

'Did you know that someone's been stealing drugs from other institutions as well?' said Willi.

'Yeah, I heard that. I know a guy at Plavack Pharmaceuticals. Some of the same drugs, but some different ones too. And always small quantities. Maybe they're inventing new intoxicants, new stimulants, new depressants. Who knows what they're up to?'

'Any ideas?' said Willi.

'Not really. Maybe it's nothing. Or like I said, new compounds for . . . I don't know what. Maybe it's about the *Grippe*. Maybe someone trying to invent a vaccine, a cure maybe? People are trying lots of crazy remedies.'

This was true. Willi himself had been treated with a tincture of creosote, coffee enemas, and something else he couldn't remember.

'Could just anybody be doing this compounding?' said Willi.

'Well, they'd have to know something, have some rough idea of what they're doing, and they'd need a lab.'

'And what would a lab need in the way of equipment?' said Willi.

Samuel reeled off a list of items, half of which Willi had never heard of. But centrifuge and scale were both on the list.

'So, someplace like a university lab, for instance?' said Willi.

'Sure. But then everybody would know what they're up to. There'd be money in it. Really big money. And if they came up with it in the university lab, then the university would get the lion's share of the profits. I'd bet that you're looking for one guy alone in a private lab.'

A SCIENCE LESSON

Doctor Ottmar von Fischer was expecting Willi. 'Come in, Detective.' The two men shook hands. 'I was just about to have some coffee,' he said. 'Would you like some?' Willi said he would.

Doctor von Fischer took two china cups from a drawer and poured coffee from a beaker sitting over a Bunsen burner. The university's Theodor Drunz laboratory was spacious and bright. A steel counter, with dozens of drawers and cabinets underneath and various equipment on top, ran down the center of the room. There were more cabinets along the facing wall. Thick books were open here and there. There were several microscopes, scales, an autoclave, three different-sized centrifuges and a few other items that Willi recognized from browsing through medical catalogues.

There was a tall apparatus at the end of the counter with wires and hoses attached, and something that looked like a small oven. There were, of course, racks of test tubes and vials and beakers with glass pipettes leading to other beakers. The opposite wall had a double sink, more drawers and cabinets, and in one corner what looked to be a shower.

A man in a white coat sat at a desk at the far end of the room, his back to them. The wall above him contained what looked to be logbooks. He had several such books open in front of him, and he was writing in a notebook.

'You have a shower in your laboratory?' said Willi.

'We deal with volatile and toxic chemicals, Detective. You spill some of this stuff on you,' said the doctor with a wave of his hand and a laugh, 'and you're in trouble. So the shower is for emergencies.'

'Is this lab yours alone?' said Willi.

'No, of course not,' said the doctor. 'A dozen doctors share it, and Freudenheim there and nine other researchers and technicians.' Freudenheim did not give any sign that he had heard his name mentioned.

The doctor sat down. He motioned to Willi to take the seat facing him. They sipped their coffee.

'This is very good coffee,' said Willi.

'Thank you, Detective. If I don't know anything else, I know coffee. Now,' he said, 'what can I do for you?'

'Is everybody who is using this lab working on the same research?'

'This is a medical lab, Detective, which means it's being used to conduct all sorts of different medical tests on samples taken from different patients. Yes, it's also a research lab for some. But I use it mainly for medical tests, blood tests, urine samples, that sort of thing.'

'Do you have a specialty, Doctor von Fischer?' said Willi.

'I'm a surgeon, Detective. But I do general medicine when it's needed. For instance, my work as part of the team of prison doctors, which is why I gather you're here.'

'What happens here in the lab, Doctor, when there's a problem with a piece of equipment – say a microscope that's broken? How do you get a replacement?'

'The university hospital has a procurement office. The head technician of the university's laboratories, Herr Erzberger, submits a request, and if the money's there, they buy it.'

'Is the money usually there?'

'Yes, it is. Medical research has a very high priority these days.'

'Because of the *Spaniche Grippe*?'

'That, yes, but also because there are many scientific break-throughs being made. It is an exciting time to be doing medical research.'

'What sorts of breakthroughs?'

'Well, there's the recent discovery that there are four different types of human blood. The discovery that there are things called vitamins in food. Do you know what vitamins are? Different foods provide different nutrients that your body needs to function as it should and that were unknown until a few years ago. And since Darwin and Galton, we are learning how human genetics plays a critical role in who thrives and who does not. There are maladies that are genetic, that some of us inherit while others do not.'

'Do you ever repair laboratory equipment?'

'No. Repair is usually more expensive than replacement, and less reliable. Besides, we don't have the people to do the repairs.'

'And when you're replacing a piece of equipment, what happens to it?'

'Usually we give it to a lesser institution, a small medical lab, or a research facility.'

'How do you find them?'

'They apply to get cast-off equipment. We make sure they have a legitimate need before giving anything away.'

'I think you took care of a prisoner at Stadelheim, Herr Doctor, a man named Gabek. He got ill and died rather suddenly.'

The doctor reached for the file on the counter beside him. 'Ladislaw Gabek,' he read. 'Forty-three years old, single, resided at 77 Aiblingerstraße. Cause of death, *Spanische Grippe*. He was already quite ill when I first saw him.'

'He died very suddenly,' said Willi.

'The *Grippe* works like that,' said the doctor. 'It is both cruel and merciful in that way.'

'How do you mean?' said Willi.

'Well, it is cruel in its manifestations, and merciful in that it is quick.'

'I see,' said Willi. 'I hadn't thought of it that way. What were the manifestations in Gabek?'

'Well, to put it in laymen's terms, his lungs were infected, causing them to fill with fluid, which made it difficult for oxygen to get into his blood. Without oxygenated blood, his vital organs could not function and they shut down. He did not suffer.'

'Did you treat him?'

'No. There was no need to treat him. Nothing could be done.'

'You didn't administer any medicine, give him any injections of anything? Any painkillers?'

'No. No injections, no painkillers. As I said, Detective, he did not suffer.'

'Were you with him when he died?' said Willi.

'No, I wasn't.'

'But you're certain he didn't suffer? How can you be sure?'

'It was over quickly,' said the doctor. He sipped his coffee.

'Gabek had been in prison for a while,' said Willi. 'Was this the only time he required medical attention?'

'According to the record, yes, the first and only time.'

'How do you suppose he caught the *Grippe*?'

'He had regular contact with guards and other prisoners. The *Grippe* is very infectious and easily communicated, that much we know. It is an opportunistic killer. It finds those who are the weakest constitutionally and takes them.'

'The weakest constitutionally?'

'Yes. You see, this brings us back to one of the medical break-throughs I mentioned, the genetic nature of disease. You could say there are those with a constitutional predisposition to get sick, a predisposition to carry disease. Disease carriers.'

'You think some humans are predisposed to illness, are disease carriers?'

'It is not a matter of belief, Detective. That is a scientific fact.'

'I'm not sure I understand, Doctor.'

'Some people are more susceptible to disease than others, Detective. They have an inherited weakness while others have an inherited strength, a resistance to disease.'

'So, Gabek had an inherited weakness that predisposed him to get sick?'

'Yes, I think he did,' said the doctor. He poured more coffee from the beaker into his cup. 'Another cup?' he said.

'No, thank you,' said Willi.

'It is a fact, Detective, that there are varieties of humans. Some, like you and me, are born of better stock. We are naturally physically stronger, more resilient, with higher intelligence, an advanced capacity for reasoning. Others come from lesser stock. They have physical, emotional, and mental deficits that have been passed down to them from their forebears. The more fit are destined to prevail, the less fit are destined for oblivion. We know this from Charles Darwin. Do you know the work of Charles Darwin?'

'I know the name, Doctor. And you're saying Gabek was of lesser stock?'

'Do you know about the science of eugenics, Detective?'

'No, I don't,' said Willi.

Doctor Ottmar von Fischer sometimes taught first-year medical students, and it was the part of his job he liked best, bringing along the next generation of students to his way of thinking. He set his coffee cup aside and steepled his fingers in front of him. Eugenics, he explained, was developed by Sir Francis Galton. It was, he said, the science of improving the human species by eliminating undesirable genetic traits, like poverty, mental illness, criminality, feeble-mindedness. This could be done in various ways, for instance, by selective breeding – encouraging those of sound stock to marry and have children, and discouraging those of inferior stock, those who were mentally or physically impaired, from reproducing.

'So,' said Willi, 'poverty and criminality are inherited?'

'Yes, of course. I'm sure you have seen that in your work, Detective. In any case, studies have shown that to be true. The poor beget the poor, the feeble-minded beget the feeble-minded, criminals beget criminals. One generation follows another. This is science.'

'And Gabek got sick because of who he was,' said Willi.

'He got sick because he was weak, a poor human specimen, and this laid him open to infection. He was in prison, Detective, convicted of insurance fraud. Poverty, criminality, a weak constitution, moral lassitude: it is all part of the same syndrome.'

TWO GABEKS

Ladislaw Gabek had left behind a twin sister. Ludmilla Gabek earned her keep as a chambermaid to a wealthy family on the far outskirts of Munich. She had made her way to Stadelheim Prison on her day off to collect her brother's meager belongings.

Willi took a streetcar to the end of the line, then walked a kilometer on a narrow lane before he came to a grand stone mansion in a park of ancient oaks and plane trees surrounded by a great iron fence. He rang the bell at the gate and a footman dressed in livery came out and led him back to the house.

Instead of taking the stairs to the main entrance, they went down a few stairs under the broad porch and into the kitchen. The footman had Willi wait while he went to find her. Willi knew the Gabeks were twins, but he was startled to see how total the resemblance was, even down to the voice.

'I'm sorry, Frau Gabek, for the loss of your brother,' said Willi, standing as Ludmilla came into the kitchen. She thanked Willi for his kind words. She had made tea, which she carried on a tray to her room as Willi followed. The room was small and sparsely furnished. She insisted Willi sit on the only chair, and she sat on the edge of the bed, the teapot and cracked cups on the tray beside her. Everything about her circumstances was threadbare and sad.

'Do you think my brother was murdered?' she asked.

'No, I don't,' said Willi. 'I'm not here about his death. I'm here on a different case.' She seemed relieved, and he was grateful she accepted his explanation for his visit.

'Where did your brother live, Frau Gabek?'

She named the street.

'So, not 77 Aiblingerstraße?' Willi had visited the address on the death certificate – a tenement building – and had found no evidence that Gabek had ever lived there.

'Would you mind showing me your brother's things you brought home from Stadelheim?'

She got up and pulled a box from under the bed. She lifted it on to the bed and took out several books. There was a well-read Bible, books of poetry, also well read, by Heine, Hölderlin; essays by Kleist, a watch, a fountain pen.

'Are these Ladislaw's things?' Willi said.

'I guess so,' said Ludmilla. 'They said they were.'

'You're not familiar with them?'

'Not really,' said Ludmilla.

'Not the watch?'

'I didn't know he owned a watch.'

'Did it surprise you when they said these were your brother's things?'

'Yes,' she said. 'I didn't think he would have books. Why would he? He couldn't read.'

'Was he a religious man?'

'We were brought up in the Church,' she said.

'Catholic?'

She nodded and, as if to prove it, crossed herself.

Willi opened the Bible and found on the title page the hand-written words, 'Praise God from whom all blessings flow. Amen.' The other books had extensive notes in the front and back and in the margins, all in the same hand as the blessing in the Bible.

'Could Ladislaw have written any of this?' he said.

'He couldn't write his own name.' She started to cry. 'He was a good man, Herr Detective. He shouldn't have been in prison. He didn't do anything bad. He just got in over his head, and now he has paid the price.'

'Over his head?' said Willi. 'How?'

'I don't know, but he said that when I saw him. He was scared, really scared.'

'When did you last see him?' said Willi.

'Right before the trial.'

'What did you mean, he paid the price? Do *you* think he was murdered?'

'He was a good man,' she said. 'Good at his job, and now he's dead.'

'His job at the printer's?' said Willi.

'No. The other job, the one with the doctors. He told me, "Ludi, I'm in too deep."'

'In too deep? What was his work with the doctors?'

'He didn't tell me. But he was a good mechanic, you know. He could fix anything. I think it was something to do with that.'

It was as if there were two Gabeks. The real Gabek: Ladislaw, the mechanic who couldn't read or write and was caught up in something sinister and had died for it. And the other 'Gabek,' with the well-thumbed Bible and the books of poetry.

The death certificate Doctor von Fischer had signed not only had the wrong address for Gabek, but it was dated the morning of the day Willi had visited him in prison. Was that a deception or just a careless error?

The real Gabek had wounds that looked like injection sites that von Fischer had either not noticed or had lied about. Or had he certified the death of the other 'Gabek' without knowing he was being used in a deception? Had the other 'Gabek' been made to vanish at the same time as the mechanic, so that one death could be used to conceal the other?

That night, Willi sat on the floor by the fire. He drew a map of this entire preposterous business – the Gabeks, one and two, side by side, with lines from each of them to Stadelheim Prison. And then Ludmilla, with a line to Gabek 1. He listed Schäuble, Erzberger, Samuel Raschermann, von Fischer on the map. He drew a line from Gabek 1 to von Fischer and wrote 'Eugenics' on the line. He wrote down 'Insurance Fraud' and drew a line to Gabek 1. He drew a line from von Fischer to Stadelheim. Then he crumpled the whole thing into a ball and threw it into the fire.

That night Willi slept on the couch in front of the smoldering embers, with Puck sleeping on his chest. Willi dreamed of an endless parade of Gabeks emerging in step from the mouth of a gigantic medical apparatus, whirring and clicking and spitting out Gabeks.

GERMANY FOR THE GERMANS

On his walk to the streetcar each morning, Willi passed the old train station building where Karlo had accosted him that time. It had not been so long ago, but it already seemed like a lifetime. The station had recently been appropriated as a kind of neighborhood headquarters by the German Workers' Party, a paramilitary/political party rising in prominence and battling various other groups for power. They had removed the boards from the windows. They had put sandbag fortifications around the place just in case. The old posters had been scraped off and every available surface was now plastered with German Workers' Party posters. Some condemned the ruinous Versailles Treaty and the socialist traitors that had facilitated it. Another pictured a boot crushing a hammer and sickle labeled 'the communist menace.' There were painted slogans – Germany for the Germans! Wake Up

Germany! – and announcements for rallies and gatherings with speeches by movement luminaries.

Young men came and went, some in brown uniforms, some wearing student colors. They carried armloads of handbills or picked up the latest issue of the *Münchener Beobachter* (Munich Observer), the party newspaper. One handed Willi a newspaper as he passed. 'Look it over, *Kamerad*,' he said. 'Don't be fooled. Learn how the Jews are poisoning our pure German bloodline.'

Willi took the paper. On the front page was a drawing of a grotesque figure, a slobbering, black-clad giant with a hooked nose, wolfish grin, bags of money in his hands, and a huge Star of David on his back. Willi was on his way to meet Gerhard Erzberger, the head laboratory technician who oversaw the university laboratories and had fired Samuel Raschermann. 'Thanks,' he said. He folded the paper and stuffed it in his pocket.

'Read it!' said the man, as Willi walked off.

Erzberger had offered to meet Willi in the Gasthaus zum Schlehdorn, a student hangout near the university. Despite the early hour, it was full of noisy and energetic young men. Nearly every table was taken. Men came and went, greeting one another, many wearing fraternity colors, caps and sashes. Willi stood in the door, looking around.

'Herr Geismeier?'

Willi turned.

'I'm Gerhard Erzberger,' said the man just behind him. He clicked his heels together and gave Willi his hand. 'Hope I didn't startle you, Herr Geismeier. Have been on the lookout for you. I realized too late the place would be busy, and you wouldn't find me easily.'

Erzberger was slight and probably about thirty, although his primness made him look older. He wore his suit jacket buttoned up, a narrow tie, his hair slicked back with pomade, and a little pencil mustache the length of his narrow mouth. He had a red and yellow fraternity ribbon on his lapel. '*Olympia*,' he said when he saw Willi noticing it.

'I work right around the corner, but I'm not usually here this early in the day. Not since I was a student. They're all getting their morning coffees or, as you see, beer for some of them.' He pressed his lips into a sour smile. 'Lamentable, I know. Men starting their day drunk.' He tut-tutted and shook his head. 'They're mostly *Nibelungia*; they're known for that. Not serious students. Let's see if we can find a place.' He looked around, spotted a small table almost behind the bar, and made a beeline for it.

Willi followed. *Good*, he thought, *he likes to talk.*

Willi sat down while Erzberger went to the bar and came back with two cups of coffee.

'I've never met a detective before,' said Erzberger. 'Must be a little like being a scientific researcher. Looking for the elements of reality, or something like that.'

'Something like that,' said Willi.

'I understand you're here about the stolen drugs,' said Erzberger. 'No need really, since we know who the villain is. Still, I'll be happy to answer your questions as best I can. We fired the thief, you know. He'll never work again. Maybe he's learned his lesson, although I doubt it. His sort never do. Quite honestly, though, I don't see the need for your investigation.'

'Even if you think you know *who* stole the drugs, there's the matter of *why* they were taken,' said Willi.

'Is that even a question?' said Erzberger. 'No, I think not. Raschermann is an addict. Used them or sold them, probably both.'

'Do you know that to be the case?' said Willi.

'Yes, I'm quite sure of it,' said Erzberger.

'Tell me more,' said Willi.

'Well, it's obvious, isn't it?' said Erzberger. 'He had access, he had opportunity, and he certainly had motivation – his own addiction and money. And, to clinch the deal, he's the type, isn't he?'

'What type is that?' said Willi.

'Well . . . defective,' said Erzberger.

'Are you referring to his infirmity?' said Willi.

'His deformity, what you call his infirmity, is a physical manifestation of his weak constitution, ergo, his inferiority,' said Erzberger. There was that phrase again.

'What do you mean by weak constitution, Herr Erzberger?' said Willi.

'Please, Detective, no need to be coy. I mean: Samuel Raschermann is an Israelite.' He nodded his head in the direction of Willi's jacket pocket, where the newspaper was sticking out. 'I know it's your job to appear objective, Herr Detective. But we have to be clear-eyed about things, don't we? We have to keep the greater good in mind. We have to see that the unfit are not allowed to pollute our German stock.'

'So, you had him fired because he's a Jew?' Willi regretted saying the words as soon as they were out of his mouth.

'I can't say that,' said Erzberger. 'You know I can't say that. But it's the same among the police, isn't it? You take certain actions, measures, precautions that have to be taken, after all, even without actually naming them?'

Willi took the newspaper from his pocket and laid it on the table. JEWS ARE KILLING CHRISTIANS IN BAVARIA was the headline under the drawing. 'Samuel Raschermann may be a Jew,' said Willi, 'but he isn't the thief. My job is to find the actual thief.'

'Why? What does it matter who stole the drugs?' said Erzberger. 'The theft was, perhaps . . . an opportunity. And for all you know, the drugs may have been put to a good use.'

'What do you mean "an opportunity?"' said Willi.

'Nothing, really,' said Erzberger. Now it was his turn to regret having spoken.

'Do you know of some particular purpose they might be used for? Do you have something in mind?' said Willi.

'No, I don't.'

'I'm not a scientist or a doctor,' said Willi. 'Give me the benefit of your experience and knowledge.'

'I have no idea,' said Erzberger.

At a nearby table, voices were suddenly raised in argument. As the argument grew louder, someone at the table started singing. It was the Olympia way: when things got heated, you started singing, everyone joined in, and that way the disputation was ended. A dozen or so men began pounding the table in time. When the song reached its final note, the room erupted in a great cheer.

'*ES LEBE HOCH DAS VATERLAND! HOORAH!*'

'You see, Detective? This is who we are now,' said Erzberger, his eyes glittering with excitement, as though the song had been his doing. 'This is the new Germany. *Deutschland gehört den Deutschen.* Germany belongs to the Germans.'

EUGENICS

D octor Aaron Trevelius had been the Geismeier family doctor since before Willi had been born. He had seen the family through one ordeal after another – Willi's childhood diseases, his father's depression, his mother's two miscarriages. Trevelius had always been there, even when there was little he could do beyond offering comfort.

He was happy to see Willi again, now looking fit and strong. They had not seen one another since Willi's parents had died. The two men shook hands. 'You look wonderful,' said the doctor.

'I couldn't help noticing,' said Willi, 'that you're packing.'

'We're moving back to Amsterdam,' said Trevelius.

'You think the situation here is that bad?'

'I don't know. But I'm afraid it will be before very long. Let's go outside for a minute; I want to show you something.' They walked back down the hall and out on to the street. Trevelius turned and pointed at the garden wall. Someone had painted a six-pointed star and written *Jude* in black paint. 'There have been other incidents,' he said. 'I can stand this nonsense. But I have to think of my wife and her parents. I can't put them at risk. We have to go.'

'I understand,' said Willi. 'But I'll be sorry to see you go.'

'Me too,' said Trevelius. 'But that's not why you wanted to see me, is it?'

'No,' said Willi. 'I want to ask you some questions about a case I'm working on.'

'Really?' said Trevelius. 'Good.' His face lit up and he rubbed his hands together.

Trevelius was still seeing patients. His office had not been packed up yet, but there were already boxes of books in one corner, and pictures had been taken off the walls.

'Sit down,' said Trevelius. 'I'll make us some tea.'

The two men sat facing one another and sipped their tea.

'I've got a puzzling case, and I was hoping you could help me,' said Willi.

'Tell me,' said Trevelius. 'I'll help if I can.'

'This case,' said Willi, '. . . I don't really know what it has to do with. I know that sounds odd. But all I've got are minor crimes that suggest major wrongdoing. Trouble is I don't have any idea what the major wrongdoing might be. At first it was just two separate cases – one about stolen drugs and maybe stolen medical equipment and another about insurance fraud. But the more I looked into it, the more the two kept running into each other in strange ways. Although I'm not even sure about that.'

'What do you mean?' said the doctor.

'Many of the people I have interviewed in both cases are scientists and doctors. Laboratory technicians and researchers too. Some have brought up what I guess you could call racialist issues. They talk about things like human stock and genetic purity.'

'I see,' said Trevelius.

'I know all that stuff is in the air these days,' said Willi.

'Yes,' said Trevelius. 'It's swirling around like the *Spanische Grippe*. You just have to breathe it in and it infects you. It's as if all anyone can think of is who's better, who's worse, who's fit, who's unfit, who's strong, who's weak, and of course who's German and who's a Jew.'

'It may be a coincidence that the people I interview keep bringing this stuff up,' said Willi. 'I don't know. It has surprised me to hear this kind of talk from doctors. Do medical people talk this way now?'

'Yes and no,' said Trevelius. 'Do you know anything about eugenics?'

'Not really,' said Willi. 'But a doctor I questioned just gave me a little lecture on it.'

Trevelius went over to the boxes of books. He looked inside one box after another until he found the book he was looking for. 'Francis Galton, *Inquiries into Human Fertility and its Development*,' he said and held up the book. He opened it and read '"*the science of improving human stock, which is by no*

means confined to questions of judicious mating, but which,
especially in the case of man, takes cognizance of all influences
that tend, in however remote a degree, to lend the more suitable
races or strains of blood a better chance of prevailing speedily
over the less suitable than they otherwise would have had. The
word eugenics would sufficiently express the idea."

'So Galton wants to manipulate every aspect of human society
so that the "more suitable" races can "prevail speedily over the
less suitable." This eugenics, as he calls it, pretends to be
scientific but there is very little scientific about it. It's a racialist
strategy and nowadays it is flourishing worldwide, especially in
England and the United States.

'Now, improving the human race is a good idea. What could
be wrong with eliminating diseases, making the human constitution stronger and more resilient, eliminating conflict and war? But
that isn't where eugenics takes us. And it's not new; it goes back
a long way and has venerable origins. Plato wrote in his *Republic*
about the value of choosing the best human specimens to produce
children and forbidding reproduction in inferior people, and
killing their offspring if they didn't comply. At one point, Roman
citizens were required by law to kill their children if they were
deformed. In my opinion, there's a straight line between this
ancient and essentially barbaric frame of mind and Galton's
eugenics.'

The two men sat in silence for a while. Then Willi said, 'So,
people I interviewed talked about finding some people inferior
because of their race or origin. No big surprise there. But one
described poverty as a genetic condition. *That* was new to me.'

'That is exactly where eugenics leads,' said Trevelius.

'The guy that said that is a medical doctor,' said Willi.

'A physician?' said Trevelius. 'Are you sure?'

'A highly placed physician,' said Willi.

'That's outrageous,' said Trevelius. 'He should be reported
to the Medical Licensing Board.'

'This is why I have come to you, Doctor.'

'Give me the man's name,' said Trevelius. 'I will look into it . . .'

'No, Doctor Trevelius. That's not what I meant. I want you to
help me understand this: to what extent, if any, is this stuff – this

eugenics – a legitimate part of modern science, of modern medical practice? And if it is legitimate medical practice, what does the practice look like? What does it entail?'

'And you think this has to do with your case?' said Trevelius.

'I don't know,' said Willi. 'This is what I'm trying to figure out.'

'Listen to this,' said Trevelius. He read from a newspaper clipping that had been folded inside the Galton book. *"Doctor Alfred Ploetz wrote his study* Racial Hygiene Basics *in 1895. Ploetz wrote that society must avoid "counterselective forces" such as inbreeding and free healthcare for the poor.'*

'Counterselective?' said Willi.

'He's referring to Darwin,' said Trevelius. 'Eugenics seems based on a willful misunderstanding of Charles Darwin's *On the Origin of Species*. What strikes me here is that Ploetz sees inbreeding and free health care for the poor as of the same order. Just like inbreeding, health care for the poor should be eliminated in order to improve the "race."'

'That's like the doctor I interviewed,' said Willi. 'He said poverty is genetic.'

'That's right,' said Trevelius. 'It's not poverty they want to eliminate, it's the poor.'

'How widespread do you think this kind of thinking is among scientists and medical doctors?' said Willi.

'Widespread enough,' said Trevelius. 'And once they're thinking that way, what prevents them from seeing physical stature or culture or race or even certain political attitudes as genetic and "counterselective" as well? Once you believe man is perfectible and you set about perfecting him, that road leads straight to hell.'

'Here's another question,' said Willi. 'If eugenics is regarded as a branch of medicine, is there some sort of "treatment" being done? If it's science, is there experimentation that goes along with it? I've heard of doctors measuring people's skulls, feeling the knots on their heads, photographing and comparing their shapes, their faces, their posture, that kind of thing. Do you think there are other more sinister things going on?'

'Heaven forbid,' said Trevelius.

'And if there are,' said Willi, 'what would such treatments, such experiments look like? What would they be trying to "cure," what would they be trying to find out, what would they be trying to prove?'

OTTMAR FREIHERR VON FISCHER

octor Ottmar Freiherr von Fischer could have told Willi and Trevelius in a few words what they were failing to understand: that the purpose of science was to lead the human race to its perfection by means of rational selection. Of course, he could not speak that way with the likes of Willi or Trevelius. They were not at his level, not capable of the long view, and thus, not devoted, as he was, to the preservation and elevation of the German race through science. If Germany was to be restored first to the Germans and then to its rightful place at the pinnacle of civilization, Ottmar believed that he would be instrumental in achieving that goal.

Ottmar had come by his perverse views honestly. He was the only son of a brutish and alcoholic father – Otto Freiherr (count) von Fischer – who believed in a sort of Germanic godliness, and an artistic mother who made paintings no one ever saw and wrote poetry no one ever read. Ottmar had grown up on an estate in East Prussia. As his father had taught him, the surrounding villages were populated by Poles and Jews, dull and grasping peasants, who, beyond the brute labor they were capable of, were essentially worthless.

They worked the land on the count's estate, but they stole what they could as they did – grain, chickens, money, anything. 'They'd slit our throats given the chance,' said Otto, who always carried a whip and a pistol when he went among them. When Ottmar became too close with playmates – peasant children – and failed to see they were as dull and without ambition as their parents, his father admonished him. 'That Petrov you like so much, he only wants what you have, and if you are not constantly on guard, he will rob you. Just wait and see.'

Count Otto left a small tart on a table while he and Ottmar watched from the doorway. Little Petrov – who had not eaten all day – broke off a piece and stuffed it in his mouth. Count Otto grabbed him by the neck. He handed Ottmar a switch and commanded that he beat the boy. 'Do it,' said Count Otto, 'or I'll beat both of you.'

As soon as Ottmar was old enough, he was sent to a boarding school where the so-called Germanic values – discipline, obedience, honor – were emphasized. From there Ottmar went off to Tübingen to study medicine with the great Doctor Erich Jaeckel, a racialist and pioneer in eugenics.

Doctor Jaeckel had written many ground-breaking articles and several books. He advised Ottmar to concentrate on genetic disorders, which he did. Needing a traditional medical specialty in order to succeed, Ottmar also trained as a surgeon. It seemed like what he was meant to do. When other young candidates were fainting in anatomy class, Ottmar wanted to cut deeper. The sight of a flayed human body excited him, the sensation of cutting flesh made him feel triumphant.

Ottmar took an anthropology doctorate along with his medical degree. His dissertation was entitled 'A Morphological Examination of the Nasal Bone in Four Racial Groups.' He proved, at least to his professors' satisfaction, an essential physical difference in the races. It was a case of 'science' backing up his deepest and firmest convictions. He believed with his whole being that white Christian Europeans, such as he and his family, were in imminent danger of being replaced by inferior races.

Jaeckel's disciples were in great demand. They readily found their way into academic and medical institutions all over Germany and were already exerting outsize influence, heading departments and research labs, founding institutes in Bonn, Frankfurt, Dresden, Hamburg and – most recently – in Vienna.

Herr Professor Doctor Wilhelm August Schäuble was no admirer of Doctor Jaeckel. Having worked his way up from poverty by dint of good, hard work, Schäuble found Jaeckel's inclination toward eugenics reckless and prejudiced and based on sloppy science. And so, for the longest time, there was no

Jaeckel acolyte on the staff of Ludwig Maximilian Hospital or on the medical faculty either. Still, Jaeckel was determined that one of his students should be on the faculty at Munich, and the opportunity finally presented itself in July of 1914 when Europe went to war.

Within weeks, six members of the medical faculty in Munich were drafted into the Army Medical Corps and sent off to the front. The university hospital found itself dangerously understaffed and therefore obliged to hire temporary replacements as quickly as they could. Because the same thing was happening at other hospitals, there were few candidates available. Doctor Ottmar von Fischer, who somehow had avoided the general call-up, presented himself as a candidate.

'You understand this is a temporary position,' said the chief of surgery. 'It will last only until the war is over and our permanent staff returns.'

'Yes, Herr Doctor, I understand,' said Ottmar. 'Thank you for considering me. I deem it a rare privilege to be associated with such a great hospital and university as the Ludwig Maximilian. I'm sure there is much I can learn from you and Professor Doctor Schäuble and the other eminent scientists on this staff.'

The chief of surgery was impressed. Doctor Schäuble, on the other hand, saw right through Ottmar's flattery. It didn't matter. The fact was they needed a junior surgeon right away and they had little choice. And since the position was temporary and everybody was sure Germany would win the war in a few weeks and all the doctors who had shipped out would come home, this Doctor Ottmar von Whoever-He-Was would soon be on his way somewhere else.

Of course, it didn't turn out that way; the war didn't end quickly. Of the six doctors who had gone off to war, two were killed when the field hospital where they were sawing off limbs and stuffing bandages into sucking chest wounds was struck by incendiary shells, killing almost everyone inside. Two others went mad, one right away, the other after a year doing triage and improvised surgery. At least it was supposed he went mad, although the bullet he put through his brain didn't leave enough of that organ behind to make a certain diagnosis. The last two doctors – friends when they had gone off to different frontline hospitals – came back intact, embraced each other joyfully, and opened a private clinic that specialized in the new science of plastic surgery, manufacturing noses and ears out of flesh borrowed from buttocks or wherever it could be spared, and stitching torn faces back together as best they could.

Ottmar stayed through the war and beyond and became highly regarded as a surgeon. He dared the riskiest procedures without hesitation. Some of the students referred to him, not to his face, as the ice man. It couldn't be disputed that he saved many lives, although he gave the impression that doing so wasn't what surgery was about for him.

He was also a brilliant teacher – strict but congenial, always willing to make time for a student with questions, just as he had been willing to make time for Willi. His teaching was along conventional and traditional lines. But genetic – that is to say, eugenic – research was his passion, not to say obsession.

Ottmar read everything available about genetic theory and experimentation. He designed his own experiments. Most remained thought experiments, since they would have been forbidden by contemporary ethics and morality. He was certain that when he was finally permitted to do them, they would demonstrate with absolute certainty the predominance of heredity in determining human identity, fortitude and intelligence. For the time being he made do with the more conventional measurements of skulls and other body parts. He had patients fill out questionnaires, he conducted interviews, and filled notebooks with his observations.

The trouble was all this measuring and asking only got you so far. It was all observational and not adherent to the hard, irrefutable rules of reproducible scientific study. You could put subjects of different racial types through various tests over and over, have them perform intelligence tasks again and again, and no matter how often the superior types succeeded and the inferior types failed, the doubters, the misguided defenders of the inferior races, dismissed the results as 'mere opinion,' 'totally subjective,' 'scientifically meaningless.'

Ottmar did take blood samples, urine samples, nasal and oral swabs when the opportunity presented itself. He smeared the samples on slides and examined and compared them through a microscope. He added various chemical substances and bacteria to the slides and examined them again. He tested and studied them every way he could, but that didn't take him far enough either. He thought drawing blood and taking samples from everyone who entered the hospital and analyzing those samples in search of racial characteristics could be an important step, but even that went too far for contemporary mores.

The principles on which eugenic science was based could never be adequately tested, much less applied. Even the steriliz-ation procedures, necessary as they were, and based as they were on genetic science, were met with public disgust, thanks to the ignorance of not just the masses but his colleagues as well. Humankind was deadlocked, held to its lowest possibilities. What was needed was better experiments, reproducible studies, biolog-ical proofs. The means were there, but there was little appetite for it.

Society needed stern measures to keep the inferiors from breeding, for they instinctively multiplied. Yet efforts at steriliz-ation or legal restriction were resisted by the misguided do-gooders. They knew better in their heads but let their so-called compassion run away with them. Many medical people felt as Ottmar did about the pollution of their German blood. They admitted as much when you pushed them in private conversation. But when it came to research, there were limits they were unwilling to cross.

AN UNHOLY ALLIANCE

Ottmar had met Gerhard Erzberger one day when Erzberger was inventorying one of the university's several labs. They struck up a conversation about research and he saw, after some cautious probing, that he and Erzberger were of one mind on racial matters. Unlike Ottmar, Erzberger was a political man, a devout anti-communist, a fan of the most virulent right-wing militias, and particularly of this young Adolf Hitler, the nationalist firebrand Munich was talking about. Erzberger believed that Germany could be saved by a revolution overthrowing the socialist regime and vanquishing the communists.

Ottmar listened, but insisted he was not political and all of that was somebody else's business. To his way of thinking, his experiments would be pure science and must therefore be kept apart from all politics, if they were to be widely accepted.

Gerhard thought, *here is a useful idiot.* He invited Ottmar to his home one evening for dinner. Gerhard lived in a luxurious apartment on the top floor of a prestigious building in the shadow of the Frauenkirche. The wood-paneled walls gleamed in the candlelight. The furniture was heavy dark wood, crimson velvet and leather. A fire flickered in the fireplace, above which hung a medieval painting of a blond Jesus, a sword in his hand and his foot on the neck of a swarthy, hook-nosed Satan.

Gerhard Erzberger had invited fifteen like-minded men. Father Johannes Kundse, the executive assistant to the Archbishop of Munich, was there. So was an army general with an eye patch, a wooden hand, and an iron cross on his lapel. Two newly inducted members of the Reichstag, both wearing brown uniforms, were there. There was also a chief of detectives, Moerdijk, as well as several captains of industry.

The evening started with drinks by the fire, where everyone chatted lightly about race and politics. After an hour or so, they sat down at the dinner table where a rabbit pâté on leek salad awaited them. The main course, served by two young men in livery, was a venison ragout. How, Ottmar wondered, did Gerhard afford all this – the apartment, the servers – on a laboratory director's salary when half of Germany was going hungry?

In the course of the larger discussion about the precarious, not to say hopeless state of the Germany economy, Father Kundse suddenly began ranting about 'Catholic Germany' being sapped of its strength by the 'Christ-killing Hebrew tribes and their degenerate, parasitic ways.'

'But what is to be done to stop it, Father?' said a captain of industry. He tightened his necktie and adjusted the lapels of his gray wool suit, as though getting ready to do battle.

'It is not complicated,' said one of the Reichstag members.

'Purge the socialists and communists from the Reichstag, and then drive the Jews out of Germany.'

'The Reichstag has all been duly elected,' said one of the other industrialists, a banker. 'You can't just purge them without an election.' He was wondering why he had come. The country needed cleansing all right, but the vehemence of the conversation made him uneasy.

'I think the answer lies with science,' said Ottmar. The others all turned and looked at him. 'For racial cleansing to take place, however it comes about, whatever form it takes, the German people must be convinced it is necessary. I have been designing studies that will scientifically demonstrate for all to see the evil effects of having a mixed-race society and the absolute necessity of a racial cleansing.'

There was a moment of stunned silence. 'Is that possible?' said the banker.

'So, what's holding you back?' said the general.

'Data,' said Ottmar. 'Collecting useful data is very difficult given current medical and scientific principles.'

'Principles?' said the general. 'What principles?'

'The principles governing how research is to be conducted,' said Ottmar.

One of the industrialists, Alejandro Acosta, wondered why it was difficult to collect the necessary data.

Ottmar explained the information he needed – racial, medical, personal – could not be collected without violating the principles around which contemporary medical practice was organized. These principles were hopelessly outdated, but they were codified in laws, and until the laws were changed to allow – even encourage – more modern procedures, he would, if he collected the data, be violating the law. He needed racial and personal medical data from thousands of subjects to run a serious study. And blood samples from that same group – now strictly forbidden for what he had in mind – would be all but impossible to get. Then he reiterated, 'I believe, with the proper data correctly studied, the dangers of racial mixing become irrefutable, and the cleansing of German society becomes imperative and inevitable.'

Alejandro Acosta was interested. He explained that as the founder and president of Royal Bavarian Assurance, he had received enrollment applications in the mail from thousands of people. Royal Bavarian was, while relatively new on the scene, already one of the largest insurance companies in Bavaria. And anyone applying for insurance coverage was required to answer many questions on the enrollment form.

There was no reason, Alejandro said, why Royal Bavarian's application couldn't be expanded to require racial and genealogical data, if that would be helpful to the doctor's scientific research. In fact, he said, there were sound actuarial reasons for gathering such data. He also said that he could, without much difficulty, demand that those covered by Royal Bavarian would have to supply a blood sample at some point in the process. All he required was that the doctor cover the expenses these changes to the form would incur. Would that be agreeable?

The next morning Ottmar met with Alejandro to draft the expanded application form. It grew from twenty-five to ninety-five questions, which covered medical history as before, but now also race, national and ethnic origins, and various physical characteristics and defects. A note at the bottom explained that as a condition of being insured, the undersigned agreed to provide a sample of his/her blood and a photograph of him-/herself if such were requested.

The new forms went out in response to every new request for insurance and, within a few weeks, completed revised forms with checks or money orders attached began arriving in the company post-office box. Ladislaw Gabek emptied the post-office box every afternoon and delivered the contents to Alejandro's office. Alejandro cashed the checks and passed the forms on to Ottmar.

By the time Alejandro Acosta fled to Argentina with many thousands of dollars – he had wisely converted his ill-gotten gains into dollars – Ottmar von Fischer had gotten over a thousand forms filled with useful data. He spent many hours entering it into logbooks, which he then spent more hours analyzing and studying. Several future studies suggested themselves based on these findings. Some would require blood samples. However, now that Alejandro Acosta had turned out to be a fraud, that would have to be put on hold.

THE LABORATORY

Ottmar von Fischer was delighted when he learned that the Ludwig Maximilian Hospital had contracted with the Bavarian state authorities to provide medical care for the prisoners of Stadelheim Prison. He offered to take over the program, and Professor Doctor Schäuble, seeing it as an onerous task, was glad to accept his offer. Here, Ottmar thought, was a population of criminals, degenerates, the insane – indisputably defective people – at his fingertips. When they became ill, Ottmar could justifiably draw blood, perform needle biopsies, even excisions. If a prisoner needed surgery, Ottmar could design the surgery according to his research requirements.

Ottmar would be treating prisoners in the prison clinic far removed from any outside observation or interference. The warden would have neither interest nor understanding of what was happening, so would not pose a problem. The prisoners did not have the right to give or withhold permission regarding medical procedures performed on them. Ottmar would now be free to advance his research as he saw fit. That his methods might lie outside the norms and guidelines governing medical and scientific experimentation would be irrelevant. All he needed now was his own private laboratory.

In the furthest reaches of Stadelheim Prison, beyond Section C, Block 8, where the criminally insane were housed and the warden was loathe to go, was an abandoned and forgotten annex. It was all that remained from the earlier prison that had been demolished to build Stadelheim. This annex, just a large room really, had been used back then to discipline uncooperative prisoners until they came to recognize the virtues of compliance. In view of the more enlightened practices now coming into vogue, the room, with its chains and shackles hanging from the wall, no longer served any useful or acceptable purpose.

For a time the room had been used for storage, until the door was finally locked for good. And, being stuck as it was beyond Section C, Block 8, it was eventually all but forgotten.

There was a back way into the room through a door in a small, neglected courtyard on Stettnerstraße – more an alley than a thoroughfare. The courtyard faced warehouses and was surrounded by a high stone wall with a door and glass shards and razor wire on top. Gerhard had discovered the place and took Ottmar there. Ottmar paced around the room – measuring, planning, deciding what could go where. The clerestory windows were covered in grime and cobwebs, but cleaned up would provide good light. Electricity could easily be brought in without anyone being the wiser. There was already a water spigot sticking out of the wall. Ottmar turned the handle and, after some rattling and gurgling, rusty water came out. 'This suits me perfectly,' he said.

One of the businessmen in Gerhard's group – an actual businessman, unlike Alejandro Acosta – offered to finance the construction and furnishing of Ottmar's new lab. And soon the windows were washed, broken panes were replaced, the room was cleaned out. The shackles and chains were removed from the walls, which were plastered and painted white. A workman built counters and cabinets in place.

Ottmar intended to buy all new laboratory equipment. But Gerhard thought they should use discarded equipment, so as to remain unnoticed. Ottmar saw the wisdom of this argument. Gerhard had relationships with labs around the city. And when a new piece of equipment was requisitioned by any one of them, he could easily arrange for the old apparatus to find its way to Ottmar's new laboratory.

Ladislaw Gabek had provided the post-office box for Alejandro Acosta, so when Gerhard demanded he refurbish the old equipment – a centrifuge, for instance – Gabek was in no position to refuse. And once he had been found out, tried, and sentenced for his crime, all Gerhard had to do when Gabek's skills were needed was to send a guard to fetch him.

BEELZEBUB

Ottmar conceived of the new laboratory – *his* laboratory – as a sacred space, set apart from the world, a universe unto itself, a place apart from sentimental falsehoods like the brotherhood of man, equality, tolerance, a place where pure, unadulterated truth based on pure, unadulterated science prevailed.

Ottmar von Fischer's disregard of and contempt for those he saw as his inferiors had been passed down to him through generations. These attitudes, which lay in the very fertile, humid center of what Ottmar might have called the von Fischers' genetic legacy, had put down roots and grown more easily with each succeeding generation, crowding out any sense of respect or empathy toward others that might have tried to grow there. There was no room for such things.

After all, disregard and contempt were comfortable and reassuring. They lifted Ottmar up, put him on a higher plane, gave him confidence, and confirmed the inadequacy of others – the many he despised. His self, his sense of personal satisfaction, even triumph, were defined by what he was not.

Ottmar carried these attitudes to Tübingen, where they were nurtured and enlarged upon, buttressed, intensified, and polished with scraps of madness he found in the society around him, until his truth's bright gleam had blinded him to everything else. His science – which was in fact anti-science – grew out of his perverse truth and not the other way around.

Ottmar was not unique back then and he would not be unique now. In every age there are scientists who construct their own scientific truths out of their prejudices. There are lawyers who find their version of justice in the injustices that inhabit their desires. There are political leaders who see their wish to dominate as a political necessity, supposedly beneficial to the masses.

Ottmar knew with absolute certainty that his thoughts and ideas were pure. And being a pure thinker, he was sure that he was infallible. And because his science was pure, its results would be incontrovertible and, if adhered to and followed, would lead society to a better world. Which meant Gabek now presented an impediment to the advancement of science, and therefore had to be gotten rid of.

The *Spanische Grippe* had occasionally found its way into the Stadelheim Prison. Visitors, lawyers, guards came and went, and so inevitably prisoners had been infected. But the plague had begun to subside and, at the moment there was but one single case within the prison. After agitating at a political rally, a communist sympathizer and poet named Dreyfus had been arrested, tried, and whisked off to Stadelheim. He had been held there in solitary confinement for the last year. And yet, despite his complete isolation, the plague had found its way to him, and he was suffering terribly.

Ottmar, covered in a protective gown and wearing a mask over his nose and mouth, waited while the guard, also masked, after peering through the peephole, unlocked the heavy iron door and swung it open so Ottmar could go inside. Dreyfus was skeletal, unshaven, filthy. He appeared to be unconscious. His hair had mostly fallen out and there were sores on his skull. He lay on a soiled straw mattress and was half covered with a stained and tattered blanket, his feet sticking out, one with a sock on it, the other one bare. His mouth was open wide as he struggled for air, taking raspy, ragged breaths. He would stop breathing, and when you thought he would not take another, he would gasp and snort, arch his back and gulp desperately for another mouthful of air.

Because Dreyfus wasn't getting enough oxygen, his body was blue. His temperature was very high and he was shivering. He did not have long to live. Ottmar took a syringe from his bag and drove the needle deep into Dreyfus's chest. As he pulled back on the plunger, the barrel filled with a milky fluid.

Once it was full, Ottmar withdrew the syringe, then put another into the man's arm. As it began to fill with blood – viscous and black – the man's eyes opened wide. They were red and they stared at Ottmar. 'I know you,' said Dreyfus. Then he said it again. 'I know who you are.'

Ottmar smiled at the man. 'Do you?'

'Beelzebub,' said the man.

THE EXPERIMENT

Ottmar had decided to take a bold and dangerous step for the sake of his science. The only thing holding him back had been a shortage of plague patients at his disposal. Then he realized he could create his own. He would inject prisoners with the plague he had collected from the prisoner Dreyfus, and treat them with sulfa and phenolic compounds of his own invention. He believed those he infected who were racially superior would likely recover, and those others who were genetically inferior would not. Their reaction to the injected compounds would confirm their degeneracy with scientific certainty.

This experimental protocol was so original and so radical that Ottmar was risking everything. But it would be different once the results were in. If things went as planned, and he was all but certain they would, his work would change eugenics and, consequently, all science forever. Then his radical methods would not matter. He would be celebrated for his discoveries, for his determination of racial truths, and for helping save Germany and the human race from mongrelization.

Gabek was surprised to be taken from his cell one morning – it was the day after his interview by the detective – and marched to the prison clinic, where he found Doctor Ottmar von Fischer waiting.

'Wait outside, please,' said the doctor to the guard, who did as he was told.

'Sit down, Herr Gabek,' he said.

Gabek sat down.

'Do you know what an epidemic is, Herr Gabek?'

Gabek said he did.

'Did you know, Herr Gabek, that there is an epidemic called the *Spanische Grippe* that has been raging through Europe and the world?'

'Yes, of course,' said Gabek. 'I know someone who had it.'

'Is that so?' said the doctor, sounding delighted. 'Well, it so happens, Herr Gabek, that some cases have shown up here in Stadelheim among the inmates. It spreads very rapidly, you know.'

'Yes,' said Gabek. 'I know.'

'You probably don't know, Herr Gabek, that science has now developed a preventative medicine that, once you are inoculated with it, will keep you from catching this disease. Did you know that?'

'No,' said Gabek.

'Yes. A vaccine. It comes, as I said, in the form of an injection, so if you roll up your sleeve for me, I will administer it and you will be protected.'

'No,' said Gabek. 'I don't want it.'

'Come, come, Gabek, it's not going to hurt. Haven't you ever had an injection before?'

'I said, I don't want it.'

'Herr Gabek, we're trying to prevent an outbreak here within Stadelheim that could infect lots of other people. Everyone will receive this inoculation. It's for your own good.'

'I don't want it,' said Gabek.

'That doesn't matter, Gabek. It's not your decision.' Ottmar picked a loaded syringe from the steel tray on the small steel table beside where he stood and took a step toward Gabek. Gabek jumped up.

'We can do this the easy way, Herr Gabek, or the hard way. It's your choice.'

'You can't make me,' said Gabek.

Ottmar stepped to the door and called the guard in. The guard was twice as big as Gabek and grabbed him from behind. But Gabek thrashed and kicked furiously, as though he knew his life was in danger.

It was no use. The guard was finally able to get him into a chokehold. Gabek thrashed a bit more and then went limp. Ottmar pushed his sleeve up and injected the serum he had made by combining the fluids he had drawn from the body of the prisoner Dreyfus.

Within twenty-four hours, Gabek was in respiratory distress. A guard warned the warden that the prisoner Gabek was exhibiting symptoms of the *Spanische Grippe*. The warden immediately notified Doctor von Fischer that there was an apparently new case of the *Spanische Grippe*. The doctor responded quickly, but Gabek was already failing and was in a stupor. Ottmar injected Gabek several times over the next days with increasing amounts of various compounds. 'The patient is critically ill,' he told the warden. 'I have medicated him, but I fear it is too late even for that. I do not expect him to live.'

Once Gabek was dead, Ottmar came back and drew several vials of blood. He took a scraping from inside Gabek's throat. Depending on what showed up under the microscope, he would be able to refine the compounds he injected in subsequent subjects. The more subjects he was able to study, the more he would be able to learn about the effects of his compounds on the different racial groups, as well as the malformed and degenerate, and thus the quality of their degeneracy.

'How can Gabek have gotten ill?' said the warden. 'Can you tell?'

'This *Grippe* is very contagious,' said Ottmar. 'Has he had any extended human contact in the last few days?'

'Guards, of course. He has a sister who visited, but not recently. There's that detective who interviewed him the other day,' said the warden.

'Well, he could be the one,' said Ottmar.

'Do you expect the infection to spread?' said the warden. He was starting to panic. 'I have thirteen hundred and forty-six prisoners in my care here.'

'I don't want to alarm you, but I am certain it will spread,' said Ottmar.

'What do you suggest I do?' said the warden.

'All we can do is monitor the situation closely,' said Ottmar. 'As cases arise, I will do what I can to treat the sick, and see that they do not suffer needlessly.'

Ottmar was correct. It did spread. He made sure of that. Two days later, there was another case, the next day three more, then two, then six. Ottmar was tireless, drawing blood, offering what comfort and cures he could to the afflicted.

Then, after a day of that, he returned to his laboratory and spent hours on end, peering into the microscope at an endless parade of blood-smeared slides. He would put a single drop of this or that chemical on to a blood sample, would note the reaction, and would describe the results in a large notebook devoted to that purpose.

Often the dawn would be casting its pink light through the clerestory windows on to the laboratory walls before he finally put the slides in their drawers, closed the notebook, locked everything away, and threw himself on to the couch to catch a couple of hours of sleep.

AN UNEXPECTED OUTBREAK

Munich, 14 September 1920

*A*n *unexpected outbreak of the Spanische Grippe at the Stadelheim Prison has caused the prison administration to curtail public visits, restrict exercise in the prison yard, and put a halt to all other communal activities until the outbreak has ended, this according to Warden Albert Dunziger.*

So far eighteen prisoners have been infected, eleven of whom have succumbed to their illness. The seven survivors are all in weak but satisfactory condition according to Doctor Ottmar Freiherr von Fischer, the prison's medical officer and a member of the surgery faculty at the Ludwig Maximilian Hospital.

The Spanische Grippe has now gone on unabated for nearly three years without prospect of a medical solution. The Grippe seems to be in decline in Munich, as it is in other parts of Germany, but, according to experts at the Institute for Epidemiological Research, there are still small, localized outbreaks, like the one at Stadelheim. These same experts tell us it is too soon to know whether the outbreak at Stadelheim is the start of a new wave of disease or just a medical outlier.

The disease outbreak was kept from spreading from Stadelheim Prison, according to Warden Dunziger, 'thanks to Doctor von Fischer's truly heroic efforts. At great personal risk, he treated every sick prisoner, monitored each of them closely, trying every available measure to restore each one to good health. As a result of his expertise and efforts, the illness was confined to the inmate population and no prison officers have contracted the disease, not a single guard or visitor has gotten sick.' Doctor von Fischer added, 'Sadly patients died, but this outbreak takes us one step closer to defeating this terrible plague and restoring Germany to health.'

Will laid the newspaper down and thought for a minute about what he had just read. Then he got up and walked the paper over to Ludwig. 'Read this article,' he said.

Ludwig read it. 'That's the doctor you talked to, isn't it?' said Ludwig.

'It is,' said Willi.

'So he's a hero,' said Ludwig.

'Sounds like it,' said Willi.

Ludwig laughed. 'But . . .?' he said.

'Ludwig,' said Willi, 'you like to play the horses.'

'OK, yes,' said Ludwig. 'You've been with me.'

'Yes, I have. Do you ever bet on long shots?'

'Occasionally. It depends on the horse's record. How has he run in short races, in longer races, on a muddy track, in heat, in the cold? How does he run in a crowd, where does he like to start? Who's the jock? All of that. You've been with me, Willi, you know how it works.'

'And would you ever bet on a horse that was bad in the mud in a short race, *to win in the mud in a short race?*'

'OK, Willi, get to the point.'

'What do you think the odds would be that the plague would find its way into Stadelheim Prison and infect eighteen people, with every single one of them being a prisoner and not a single guard being infected, the warden not being infected, no visitor being infected, nobody being infected except prisoners? What are the odds?'

'They kept everybody segregated,' said Ludwig. He read from the article. 'They curtailed public visits . . . restricted exercise in the prison yard . . . put a halt to all other communal activities.'

'Not right away they didn't,' said Willi. 'They couldn't do it that quickly. None of that happened while Gabek was sick. I was there. They couldn't have known they had an outbreak until they were several days in, and by then it would have been too late. Besides, I was there, Ludwig. They took me to the morgue, I talked to guards, the warden, the coroner. Nothing was curtailed. Nothing. So, what are the odds?'

TOO MANY COINCIDENCES

'A coincidence is all it is,' said Ludwig. It *had* to be a coincidence. The alternative possibility was a crime too horrible to even imagine.

'You're right, Ludwig,' said Willi. 'It's a long way from these dead prisoners to any criminal activity. There is probably a logical explanation for it that we're missing. I'm just asking questions.'

'And, besides, you're talking about lowlifes here,' said Ludwig. 'Thugs, pickpockets, rapists, a murderer.'

'They were doing their time, Ludwig; they were wards of the state. None of them was sentenced to death. No one deserves to die from this terrible plague.'

'Sorry, Willi, but come back to me when you've been doing this for forty years, rooting around in the human sewer among perverts and criminals. I guarantee, you'll feel different. Good riddance to bad rubbish, I say. Anyway, they died of natural causes. There's nothing there.'

'There's the insurance fraud . . .'

'Solved,' said Ludwig. 'The guy's in Argentina.'

'Connected somehow?' said Willi. 'And the stolen drugs?'

'Small beer,' said Ludwig.

'But there's this eugenics doctor who wants to make perfect humans, Ludwig. Doesn't that at least raise questions?' said Willi.

'Hell no, it doesn't,' said Ludwig. 'The human race could use some perfecting. Anybody knows how to do that, I'd say give it a try.'

Ove spoke up. 'That kind of thinking can lead to bad stuff, Ludwig. People who think they're better than everybody else, they think it gives them rights they don't have.'

'Not that I'm better than everybody else,' said Ludwig. 'But people don't end up in prison just because they're down on their luck. Some people are born evil and society has to deal with them. That's why we're cops, isn't it?'

'All I'm saying,' said Willi, 'is a number of prisoners are dead. I'd just like to find out why, that's all.'

'OK,' said Ove. 'Go ahead. But tread lightly, Willi. This doctor's a big hero now. They're going to give him a medal, you know. The mayor will be there. Everybody thinks he's wonderful.'

It was true: the city government, thinking people needed someone positive to celebrate, had decided to honor the lifesaving Doctor Ottmar Freiherr von Fischer with a ceremony in the city hall – speeches, toasts, and a medal.

Willi called Izabella Bauer. After a moment, she remembered Willi. 'Of course. You solved Walther Metger's murder.' She asked him about himself, how he was. He told her he had been in the war, but he left out the details. 'I'm back to being a detective. And how are you?'

She said she had married during the war and moved to Berlin for a time. But she was alone now, so she was back to being an editor at the *Kurier*. 'Managing editor, these days, which is good. How can I help you?'

'I wanted to talk to you about a story you ran, Frau Bauer,' he said. 'Front page, about Doctor Ottmar von Fischer, the prison doctor who saved the lives of all those prisoners.'

'Oh, yes,' she said. 'What about it?'

'I'm just curious about your take on that story,' said Willi.

'You mean that it was a coincidence?' she said.

'Yes, that, for one thing,' said Willi.

Izabella paused then said, 'Listen, Detective, I can't talk to you now. Could we meet for coffee?' She named a place near the *Kurier* offices.

She was waiting, smoking a cigarette, an empty coffee cup in front of her, when Willi arrived. She was prettier than he remembered, a little thinner, with streaks of gray running through her blonde hair. She stood up. They shook hands and then, to his surprise, she leaned in and kissed his cheek. Her lips were soft and warm.

Willi had to collect himself for a moment and Izabella saw his unease.

'I'm sorry,' said Izabella.

'No, no, it's fine,' said Willi. 'It's just that . . .'

'No, really, I shouldn't have . . .'

'It's fine, really.' He looked past her, out the window, at the people passing, looking for Eva's face maybe. 'Frau Bauer,' he said finally, turning back to look at her – that was the trick, call her by name. 'Frau Bauer, why were you uneasy talking on the phone . . . about the story, I mean?'

'Well, Herr Detective' – she said it without irony – 'the *Kurier* has a new owner, Robert Zweibel, and he has a habit of listening in on people's conversations. Also, it happens he's friendly with Doctor von Fischer.'

'Is that the coincidence you meant, on the phone I mean?'

'No. That's interesting, but the coincidence I was thinking of was that only prisoners got ill and died. Or were saved. No one else, just prisoners. That's what I meant. I thought that was something readers would notice that warranted further explanation if we were going to run the story, especially on the front page as we did. So I would have held it up. And to be completely honest, I thought it was a page six story. But Herr Zweibel wanted it on the front page, and right away.'

'Do you know why?' said Willi.

'He said it was important and . . . the *Kurier* was breaking the story, so that's probably why he was in a hurry. I wanted to hold it until we knew more about the coincidence.'

'And did you ever find out more about why it was only prisoners?'

'No. Nobody at the prison would talk to us. But there are a couple of possibilities. One, that it's just a coincidence: only prisoners got sick and died. That kind of coincidence can happen. Or two, guards and others got sick too, but that fact was never made known. So that's what I wanted to find out before we ran it. Do you have any ideas?'

'No,' said Willi. 'So the warden wouldn't talk to you?'

'Nobody would. Our reporter Gregor Wertheimer couldn't even get the names of the dead or the sick. Which I also find odd.'

'Is your reporter still working on it?'

'He is. What's your interest in the story, Herr Detective?'

'Well, same as yours, I think: the coincidence. Has Wertheimer ever talked to Doctor von Fischer?'

'He can't get near him either,' said Izabella. 'The whole situation is very buttoned up, which also makes me wonder. Have you ever talked to him?'

'I did once, before all the dead prisoners showed up.'

'What's he like?'

'Charming and cold as ice,' said Willi.

'Wertheimer's going to try again.'

'When?' said Willi.

'Tomorrow,' said Izabella. 'There's supposed to be a press conference after the ceremony.'

'Could you get him to ask von Fischer about Gabek?' said Willi.

'Gabek?' said Izabella.

'One of the dead prisoners,' said Willi. He told her about Gabek and the guard, about the two Gabeks, about Gabek's sudden death. 'He should ask von Fischer how Gabek died?'

'Why don't *you* ask him?' said Izabella.

'There were five injection sites on his arm,' said Willi. 'Ask him about those too.'

'Do you expect him to answer?'

'No,' said Willi, 'I don't.'

'So you're using the *Kurier*,' said Izabella.

'Yes,' said Willi.

'Hoping for what?'

'I think von Fischer's a villain, I just don't know what kind. I also think he may be part of something bigger than himself. He's a eugenicist, you know. He believes in a fairly extreme race theory.'

'Zweibel too,' said Izabella. 'That's interesting.'

'Suppose for a moment, as ridiculous as it sounds, that von Fischer killed those prisoners.'

'I'm sorry. It's not something I can even imagine. He's a doctor, for crying out loud.'

'I know,' said Willi. 'But I was handed a newspaper the other day calling for Jews to be expelled from Germany. I met another scientist who more or less said the same thing. This eugenics stuff leads to that kind of thinking. Even my partner was just saying, "good riddance to bad rubbish;" he was talking

about prisoners. Anyway, poking the hornets' nest is all I've got
right now, and I'm hoping your Wertheimer might do that for
me in a way that I can't.'

THE HERO

E duard Schmid, Munich's mayor, was being attacked
constantly from all sides, for doing too much or too little
of the right thing or the wrong thing. He needed all the
diversions his people could muster. And, as his chief of staff
pointed out one morning, laying the morning *Kurier* in front of
him, Doctor Ottmar von Fischer was just the sort of man who
could help. Fischer would soon be the man of the hour, the story
would soon be in all the papers – a heroic physician fighting the
plague and, lo and behold, saving the lives of many. 'He should
be publicly celebrated; he should be honored. A gala ceremony
would play very well.' The mayor, an astute politician, saw the
wisdom immediately.

It was a bright sunny morning, a crowd of a few hundred
people was milling around on the Marienplatz in front of the
New Town Hall. A brass band was playing marches and waltzes.

Willi was there in the crowd. Ottmar stood up on the stairs
beside the mayor, looking a little uncomfortable in his morning
coat, striped pants and spats. Gerhard Erzberger stood on his
other side. The mayor read a brief statement about the doctor's
heroic life-saving activity, his dedication to the healing profession. He thanked Ottmar profusely in glowing terms, referring
to him over and over as Herr Doctor Ottmar Freiherr von Fischer.

Finally the two men shook hands. A blue and white sash with
a gold inscription was draped over Ottmar's shoulder, and a
medal was hung around his neck. The two men clasped hands
again and held that pose, their smiles frozen, while the official
photographer took their picture.

Ottmar had decided he would not speak or, for that matter,
answer questions from the press, so the press conference had
been canceled. Still, there was a clutch of reporters just below

the stage. As Ottmar, the mayor and the other dignitaries turned to leave, the reporters began shouting questions.

'Doctor von Fischer, do you think a cure for the *Spanische Grippe* is within reach?'

'Herr Doctor, will there ever be a vaccine?'

'Doctor von Fischer, what does it feel like to be a popular hero?'

'Herr Doctor von Fischer, is this plague finally behind us?'

'How did Ladislaw Gabek die, Doctor?'

Ottmar heard 'Gabek' as he passed through the door into the Old Town Hall vestibule where the champagne reception was to take place. Gregor Wertheimer, seeing Ottmar's head swivel in his direction, shouted his next questions: 'Doctor, why was Gabek injected? What was he injected with?'

Since the name Gabek and the questions meant nothing to the others present, they were ignored and quickly forgotten by most everyone else. But Ottmar, now in the vestibule where the champagne was already being poured, and waiters in black vests and long white aprons were circulating with bits of pickled herring on little rye crackers, expressed his regret to the mayor's chief of staff. He had just been informed by his colleague Herr Erzberger of a medical emergency that required his immediate attention, a surgical procedure that could not wait another minute. As much as he regretted it – he adored champagne, he said – he would have to forgo the reception.

Mayor Schmid came over and expressed his regret, shook hands with Ottmar once more, and wished him well. Ottmar asked whether there was a back way out. The chief of staff escorted Ottmar and Gerhard to a rear entrance through which they fled. 'Hmm,' said the chief of staff to no one in particular as he watched them go. 'Some people just don't know when to seize an opportunity.'

WHAT MUST BE DONE

'I was against this whole goddamned stunt,' said Gerhard.

'Stunt?' said Ottmar.

'The Town Hall celebration,' said Gerhard. 'The publicity.'

The two men were hurrying along the street, Ottmar still wearing the gold embroidered sash, still with the medal swinging from a ribbon around his neck.

'It was science being celebrated,' said Ottmar indignantly, 'real medical science. Soon we can expand the experiment to include a larger population.'

'Soon? *Soon?* And what about the meantime, what about now when what you've done is still against the law, when your grand experiment is still considered murder! What planet do you live on? You just killed eleven men . . .'

'Eleven seriously defective men,' said Ottmar, 'while eight men of good German stock survived.'

Gerhard stared at him. He had thought of Ottmar as a useful idiot. While he was certainly some kind of idiot, he was not a particularly useful one, not at this moment anyway. 'What planet do you live on, Ottmar?' he said again. 'The world isn't ready for you to perform your experiments on living humans.'

'Not yet,' said Ottmar.

'Not *yet?*'

'But they will be. Soon they will be.'

'In any case,' said Gerhard – he saw the danger they were in – 'you have records of the . . . procedures you performed?'

'Of course, I have all the details. I have documented all my experiments. I have begun writing a paper on—'

'Where are they?' said Gerhard. He looked around, saw a taxi, and waved it down. 'Where are these details, where's the paper?'

'In the lab,' said Ottmar. 'Everything is in the lab. The samples too.'

'Samples?'

'Blood samples, excisions, it's all there, all labeled, all documented.'

'Really?' said Gerhard. They got in the cab. 'Stettnerstraße, driver, and hurry.'

'It's science, Gerhard. That is how science works. For any experiment, the protocol and procedure has to be scrupulously documented to take any experiment to the next level.'

'Listen to me, Ottmar, and listen carefully. I'm going to drop you at the lab right now, and you're going to gather together all the records of your experiments. All the records and samples,

everything, and move them all to a safe location. Everything. Do
you understand me?'

'Yes, OK,' said Ottmar. 'That is prudent. I'll move them. But
the records must be saved at all costs.' Ottmar wasn't going to
move anything. This was his life's work. He couldn't be shuffling
from one secret place to another.

They rode in silence, Ottmar absently fondling his medal and
Gerhard thinking things out. He was pretty sure Detective
Geismeier was their main problem, at least at the moment. He
found some comfort in that, since he was pretty sure Geismeier
had nothing. Nobody at the prison was talking to anybody. The
Kurier could only know about Gabek from Geismeier. And
Gerhard figured all they could have at this point, beyond wild
fantasies and ridiculous suspicions, was that Ladislaw Gabek
was one of the dead prisoners and that he had received several
injections in an apparent effort to save his life.

What could possibly be wrong with that? Nobody would
imagine that an eminent surgeon and proclaimed hero was killing
his patients. And, in fact, would anybody even care that a bunch
of criminals had died? Anyway, a false medical report signed by
von Fischer should satisfy the newspapers and lay any grotesque
rumors to rest.

Geismeier was another matter. He had to be stopped. Von
Fischer would want nothing to do with that, but Gerhard could
take care of it. He had a connection or two in the police department, including Chief of Detectives Moerdijk. And if Moerdijk
couldn't put a stop to it, he knew of people who could. Men did
that sort of thing for hire, and in today's Munich they wouldn't
be too hard to find.

At the corner of Stettnerstraße, Gerhard said, 'Stop here,
driver.'

Ottmar got out, walked to the courtyard entrance, took an old
iron key from his jacket pocket.

Gerhard watched him go inside before he instructed the driver
to take him to the university. After Gerhard drove off, Willi got
out of his cab and walked to the corner just in time to see the
courtyard gate close.

GUTTING A TROUT

The next morning Willi made an appointment to have another conversation with Doctor von Fischer in the hospital laboratory. Ottmar greeted Willi politely. Freudenheim was not in the laboratory, but two other doctors were. One wore a suit and one wore a white coat with a name tag: Doctor Strauß.

'Picking up test results, I imagine,' said Ottmar without acknowledging them.

Once they left, Willi asked who they were.

'Doctors,' said Ottmar.

'I see,' said Willi. 'I wanted to let you know, Herr Doctor, that the case of the missing drugs is expanding,' said Willi.

'Is it?' said Ottmar.

'I felt sure you would have no objection to my looking around your laboratory.'

'Do you have a search warrant?' said Ottmar. Gerhard had warned him to be careful, that Detective Geismeier could be dangerous.

'Yes, I do,' said Willi, taking it from his jacket pocket.

Ottmar studied it. He had never seen one before. 'Should I accompany you?' he said. 'In case anything needs explaining?'

'Of course,' said Willi, 'that would be a big help.' He started moving around the lab, looking inside cabinets, opening drawers. 'I see some of the cabinets are locked,' he said.

'Every doctor has his own cabinet,' said Ottmar. 'They usually keep them locked.'

'If I want to look inside, then we'd need to get each doctor to unlock his own? Or is there a master key?'

'There is a master key,' said Ottmar.

'Who has that key?'

'The senior physician, in this case, Herr Doctor Strauß.'

'The man who was just here?' said Willi.

'Yes.'

'Which is your cabinet?' said Willi.

'This one.'

'You don't lock it?' said Willi.

'I don't have much in it,' said Ottmar. 'As you can see.' He opened the door. It contained a key ring with a few keys – Ottmar grabbed it and slid it into his pocket – a coffee grinder and a few cups and saucers. There were a few papers, but all were official university notifications. There were three books – two novels and an illustrated book on surgical techniques. 'What exactly are you looking for, Detective?'

'I don't know, Doctor. It's a bit like medical research, I imagine. When something's out of place, something's off, that can indicate it needs further investigation. That's what I'm looking for: something that's out of place.'

'Aha,' said Ottmar.

'Could I look at the keys in your pocket?' said Willi.

'Why?' said Ottmar.

'Because you put them in your pocket,' said Willi.

Ottmar handed him the key ring. There were four keys. He could see none of them matched the lockers.

'What are these keys for, Doctor?'

'They're my house keys,' said Ottmar.

'All of them?' said Willi.

'All of them,' said Ottmar.

'For instance,' said Willi, continuing his answer to Ottmar's question, 'in your genetic research, if something unusual jumps out at you, an anomaly of some sort, that takes you down a particular path, doesn't it?'

'It can,' said Ottmar. As naive as he was, he could tell when he was being herded on to thin ice. 'As I told you when we last met, Detective, I use this lab mostly for blood tests. I don't have any particular research going on, which is why there's not much in my locker.'

'After you told me something about genetics, I did a little reading, Doctor. It's a fascinating field; I see why it interests you. I mean, scientists learning a man's physical or psychological profile, I guess you'd call it, from the shape of his skull, the color of his eyes . . . I know someone who has one brown and one blue eye, and there are studies . . .'

'Heterochromia iridum,' said Ottmar.

'Yes, that's it,' said Willi.

'That happens to be an interest of mine,' said Ottmar, stepping out on to the ice after all.

'I gather, just its presence can signify physiological problems. Is that correct?'

'Heterochromia comes about thanks to accidents in the distribution of melanin – the pigment in the body that we think determines race. In my opinion, heterochromia is inherited, the result of disease and or inbreeding. But that, of course, has yet to be proved.'

'How would you ever be able to prove such a thing, Doctor?'

'Scientific experimentation, Detective, would be the only way to determine the full meaning of heterochromia in an individual or a collection of individuals.'

'What kind of experiments might do that, Doctor?'

'Trying to change the coloration of the iris in subjects with heterochromia by injecting dyes, for instance: that could be a fruitful direction.'

'Injecting dyes?' said Willi.

'Into the subject's eyes,' said Ottmar. He smiled.

Willi found Doctor Peter Strauß at the front desk of one of the psychiatric hospital wards. He told him who he was and showed him his badge. 'You've heard about the drugs missing from the hospital and other laboratories, Doctor?'

'Yes,' said Doctor Strauß.

'That's what I'm here investigating,' said Willi.

'Do you need to look around this ward, Detective? You should have an escort with you, but I can tell a nurse to take you.'

'No, thank you, Doctor. I just wanted to talk to you for a moment.'

'All right,' said Doctor Strauß and laid the charts he was carrying on the counter.

'Doctor von Fischer told me, as the senior physician you have the master key to all the lockers in the laboratory where we saw each other earlier.'

'That is true,' said Doctor Strauß. 'Do you need to see inside those lockers? Of course, I'll need a search warrant from you.'

'No, not at the moment. But, I couldn't help noticing back there, Doctor Strauß, that you and Doctor von Fischer are not on friendly terms.'

'You're quite the detective,' said Doctor Strauß with a sour smile.

'Do you mind telling me why?'

'Not at all, Detective. I don't like the bastard,' said Doctor Strauß.

'Why not?' said Willi.

'Does this have to do with the case you're investigating?' said Doctor Strauß.

'Yes, actually it does.'

'Well then: first of all, he's a flaming anti-Semite,' said Doctor Strauß, 'and I am a Jew.'

'I see,' said Willi. 'You said "first of all." Anything else?'

'He's a psychopath.' Doctor Strauß waited to let that sink in. 'Do you know what a psychopath is, Detective?'

'I think so,' said Willi, 'at least in a general way.'

'Then let me be specific. A psychopath is someone whose behavior is generally amoral and antisocial. A psychopath has no conscience. None. He is incapable of empathy or compassion. There is a great void where his conscience, empathy and compassion should reside, where they are to be found in a normal human being, like you or me. A psychopath does not know shame or remorse or even understand the concepts of shame and remorse. And thus a psychopath is given to perverse and criminal behavior, since there is no difference between such behavior and normal human behavior in his understanding. Given his nature, perversion and criminality come quite naturally to him.'

'Are you saying, Doctor, that Doctor von Fischer is engaged in criminal behavior?'

'No, Detective, I'm not saying that. But I am saying he is eminently capable of it. And if he *were* engaged in criminality, he would find reasons for it, justification for it, treat it as though it were a matter of course, even a matter of necessity, and would show no regret. None. And, I should add, if he were engaged in criminal behavior, it would not surprise me at all.

'I see that shocks you, Detective. As it should. In my thirty-plus years of practicing psychiatry, I have encountered maybe two dozen true psychopaths. Every one I have met was almost immediately recognizable to me as a psychopath. There is an evident moral and spiritual void, a moral depravity that lives in them and emanates from them. If you are not frightened of Doctor Ottmar Freiherr von Fischer, Detective, you should be.'

Doctor Strauß gave Willi the name and whereabouts of his friend Doctor Albertsohn, whom Willi had seen with him in the lab. When Willi asked Doctor Albertsohn about Doctor von Fischer, he deferred to Doctor Strauß's opinion. 'I am a general practitioner,' he said. 'There's nothing I can disagree with or add to what Peter has said. You know, Detective, if you'd like to see psychopathy in action, you should watch von Fischer operate. There is a surgical theater in his building where students go to learn from the best surgeons. Fischer, a highly skilled surgeon, does operate there once in a while, and I could get you in.'

'I wouldn't know what to look for,' said Willi.

'I promise you, you would see right away, this is a man who has no regard for the person he is cutting. None. I'm telling you: I've seen students faint, doctors too. And it's not the blood that causes it, it's the surgeon. It is evident from the moment his scalpel touches living flesh. He could as easily be gutting a trout.'

THE HORNETS

Back at the precinct, patrolmen and detectives were milling around waiting for a meeting to begin.

'What's going on, Ludwig?' said Willi.

'Ove is gone,' said Ludwig.

'What do you mean gone?'

'We're being consolidated,' said Ludwig. 'With the Ninth Precinct and the Seventeenth. Ove has been fired.'

'Where is he?' said Willi.

'I don't know. He's been fired, and he's gone.'

'Did I miss something? Was there an announcement?'

'No. We just got the word an hour ago. There's a meeting at eleven.'

Finally, at eleven thirty, a civilian official, two police captains and three sergeants came marching in. One of the three was Sergeant Schobert from Willi's first days as a policeman. He was heavier now and had a shaved head. He didn't see Willi in the crowd at first.

'Let's get started, men,' said the senior captain, taking off his hat. Everybody quieted down.

'Ove Sandheim has retired,' said the captain; there was a general muttering, 'and three precincts are being consolidated. The ninth, the thirteenth, and the seventeenth. Captain Reineke will be taking over. He will be in overall charge.' The three sergeants would be running the day-to-day operation and would circulate among the three precincts.

'Where's Ove going?' somebody shouted.

'There'll be none of that,' said Captain Reineke, stepping forward, his fists on his hips. 'Suffice to say, Ove Sandheim ran a loose ship and those days are over.' There was more grumbling. 'The next one of you that makes a sound out of line is done; your days as a policeman are over. Is that understood?' The room went silent.

The sergeants looked around the room, scowling as they did. That was when Schobert spotted Willi. His eyes widened slightly; his scowl deepened. Willi's eyes met his, and Schobert looked away. *That bastard*, he thought. *Just my damn luck.*

The civilian official and the senior captain left, and the patrolmen and detectives were called in one by one to meet with Captain Reineke and the three sergeants to learn how much more difficult their lives were about to become. Of course, they were expected to stand at attention, to call their superiors sir. No more of Sandheim's cozy goings-on. The department, and this precinct in particular, would now have to toe certain political lines too and follow strict department protocols. From here on out they would be 'on a short leash,' 'held to close account.' Things were to be more 'down the line.' No one knew exactly what any of that meant, but everyone knew it was political and it sounded bad.

When it was Willi's turn, Schobert came out. 'Detective Geismeier,' he shouted, looking around the room as though he didn't know who Willi was. Captain Reineke was sitting at Ove's desk and Schobert sat down with the other two sergeants on chairs behind him. Reineke was studying Willi's file. 'How old are you, Geismeier?' he said.

'Twenty-six, Captain,' said Willi.

'Sir!' said Schobert.

'Twenty-six, Captain, sir,' said Willi.

The captain looked up to see whether Willi was being impudent. He couldn't tell. 'Twenty-six. Correct,' said the captain. 'That's damn young for a detective. Do you realize that?'

'Yes, sir, I realize that.'

'He was first in his class, Captain,' said Schobert. 'Isn't that right, Geismeier?'

'First time, yes,' said Willi. 'Not the second time, Sergeant Schobert. Sir.'

Reineke studied Geismeier again. So far, everything out of his mouth sounded impudent. This one would bear watching.

'How are your eyes, Geismeier? A detective with bad eyes doesn't seem like a good idea.' He smiled and looked to the sergeants for confirmation, and they nodded and puffed on their cigarettes. 'The war?' he said.

'Yes, sir, Captain. The war.'

'You were one of Sandheim's fair-haired boys, is that right?'

'I wouldn't know, sir.'

'You have closed a couple of important cases, I see.'

Schobert looked uneasy. Willi didn't answer.

'On the other hand, you've wasted way too much time on this drug case. I told Detective Voss already – we're dropping that case. There's nothing there, it's a waste of time. We want you to focus on real crime.' He handed Willi a folder. Willi opened it. 'Since you're such a hotshot, Geismeier, I'm going to let you take your pick of cases.'

Willi turned the pages. Somebody had been attacking communist newspapers, destroying the presses and assaulting the staff. Somebody else was selling stolen military weapons. And there was a plot to overthrow Munich's socialist mayor. All three cases were made to order to get Willi in trouble.

'We hear you're a great detective, Geismeier. So put your marvelous skills to work on one of those, would you be so kind?' He waited. Again, no response from Willi. 'Is that understood, Detective?'

'Understood, yes, sir.'

'And stop harassing the doctors, Geismeier. And stay away from Stadelheim. If I find out you've gone anywhere near them, I'll have your head on a plate. Is that understood, Geismeier?'

'Yes, sir, Captain. Understood.'

There it was. The hornets' nest had been poked.

ON THE OTHER HAND

Benno von Horvath, an old friend of Willi's father and one of Munich's police chiefs, invited Willi to meet him for lunch at Zum Dürnbräu. When Willi arrived, Benno was sitting at a table on the terrace under a flowering linden tree reading the newspaper, an empty beer glass in front of him. The bees were buzzing overhead by the hundreds. The fragrance of the flowers was heavy and intoxicating. Benno stood to shake hands with Willi. 'Are you all right with eating out here?' said Benno, waving at the tree above him. Willi said he liked the idea. Benno held up two fingers and the waiter brought them two beers.

Willi asked about Margarete, then about acquaintances they had in common. The waiter took their order and brought their food. Benno had a pork schnitzel with roasted potatoes, Willi had a sausage and kraut. Benno asked Willi how he was doing these days. Willi said he was sad, and he was lonely.

'These things take a long time to get over,' said Benno.

'I know,' said Willi. 'I'm all right, Benno. Thanks to Puck.'

'Puck?' said Benno.

'A cat,' said Willi.

'Aha. I understand,' said Benno, but he didn't.

It was a warm day. Willi took off his jacket. 'What made you decide to retire, Benno?'

'I'm sixty-five,' said Benno.

'I know that,' said Willi, 'but why'd you retire?'

Benno smiled. He knew Willi wouldn't let up until he had a real answer. It was true Benno was feeling his age, but that wasn't why he had retired. Margarete wanted him to retire. She dreamed of traveling. She wanted to see North and South America. Maybe they'd take a cruise. But that wasn't his reason either.

'I was forced out,' said Benno. 'Policing is changing. Police culture is changing. And I no longer have any part to play.'

'What do you mean?' said Willi.

'Administering the force, hiring new cops, enforcing the law, everything about policing is becoming a political act. Where you are politically, whether you're left or right plays an important part in every action, every decision. You can probably see that better than I can from your vantage.'

'What have you heard?' said Willi.

Benno smiled. Willi was always two steps ahead of everybody else. 'Willi, I have never met anyone who had a better head for police work than you. You have a gift for finding wrongdoing and, at the same time, you have a taste for justice.'

Willi was about to protest, but Benno held up his hand to stop him.

'I'm not paying you compliments, Willi. A gift like yours can be a curse in times like these. Because the more the law becomes political, the more it inevitably veers away from justice and toward wrongdoing.

'Fascism is on the rise, Willi. The terrible Versailles treaty has brought us Germans to our knees. Fascists on the right and left are using this moment to disrupt our young, fragile republic and seize power for themselves. The communists are violent and dangerous. But I'm more afraid of the nationalists. And they – the nationalists, fascists, racialists – are now in positions of power and control in our police department. And once they control the police, they will control the law.

'I was forced out, Willi, because they want someone who will help spread nationalism and anti-Semitism through the ranks. They have found their man and installed him as my successor, a German Workers' Party hack, a fan of this Hitler fellow.'

'I didn't know that, Benno. I'm sorry,' said Willi.

'Don't be sorry for me, Willi. I've had a good career. I was able to help the Munich police department find its way into the twentieth century. I don't know the particulars, Willi, and I don't want to know them. I'm not asking. But I hear you have been pursuing a case or cases that are about to land you in hot water. The fact that I've heard about it probably means you're in a bad situation.'

Willi sipped his beer. He knew, maybe better than Benno could, what a cop in the trenches was facing these days, and where things seemed to be going. But he hadn't thought about it in terms of himself, either his safety and security, or his future as a cop. It was sobering to hear Benno lay it out in such a stark way.

'What would you do, Benno, in my shoes?'

'That's a hard question for me to answer, Willi. I can't see the future. Maybe the Weimar Republic will hold together and muddle through; maybe we Germans will become reasonable again; maybe the extreme factions will wither away.'

'Yes, Benno,' said Willi, 'but what would you do if you were me?'

'I'm the wrong man to ask, Willi. After all, I've surrendered.'

STETTNERSTRAßE 11

W illi spent a few hours in the New Town Hall searching through property registries before he found what he was looking for in a volume that included architectural drawings of the prison at Stadelheim. One drawing of the old prison showed the small courtyard and the three buildings. The two buildings on either side of the courtyard – numbers nine and thirteen – could be entered from Stettnerstraße. Both were warehouses, one listed as a long-gone wine merchant, the other as Holzmeister's lumberyard which was still active.

The building at the back of the courtyard – Stettnerstraße 11– could only be accessed through the courtyard. Tax records showed that the building and the courtyard were owned by the city of Munich, and because they were not in use, they were not being taxed. 'Is there anything else you need to know about it, Herr Meier?'

Willi had signed the register as Wilhelm Meier. 'Is this

property currently promised or in use?' he said. 'And if not, is the city willing to rent it out for commercial use?'

The clerk – the sign on his desk said Herr Schlegemann – was one of those government bureaucrats who takes the term 'public servant' literally. And because most people came to him either to pay or dispute their taxes, neither of which was a very happy enterprise, a customer he could actually help, even if it was only to provide information, was a welcome relief. 'I will research your questions, Herr Meier. Come back tomorrow afternoon; I should have answers by then.'

Willi went to look at the property. The abandoned wine merchant's warehouse at number nine had no windows and only a heavy wooden door crisscrossed with iron straps facing the street. The door was chained and padlocked shut. Getting to the courtyard and number eleven that way would be impossible without attracting attention. And the wall between nine and thirteen was ten feet tall with broken glass and razor wire uncoiled along the top.

On the other hand, the door to Holzmeister's lumberyard was wide open. It was watched over just now by an older man wearing the faded blue overalls of a carpenter, which had once been his occupation. It was his job now to sit at a small desk just inside the door waiting for customers to arrive from the Holzmeister office around the corner with an invoice in hand. He would study the invoice, then disappear back into the long racks of lumber. He would re-emerge pushing a cart with the boards, panels, parquet or molding the customer had purchased.

When Willi came through the door, the man stuck out his hand. 'Invoice,' he said.

'Hello,' said Willi. 'Sorry, I just wanted a little information.'

'What kind of information?' said the man.

'I'm just curious about the courtyard next door and the building at the back.'

'What about them?' said the man.

'Well,' said Willi, 'my name is Wilhelm Meier and I might be interested in renting that building. I know it's owned by the city, but I just want to find out as much as I can about the place. You've been around here for a while, Herr . . .?'

'Meier,' said the man with a laugh.

Willi laughed too. 'Not Wilhelm, I hope,' he said.

'Fritz,' said the man, and they shook hands and laughed again. 'Well, I can't tell you much, Wilhelm. Except that lately there's been some activity back there. So maybe it's been rented to somebody else already.'

'What kind of activity?' said Willi.

'Construction,' said Fritz. 'They put in electricity, put in some cabinets. And there's been some coming and going.'

'Coming and going?' said Willi.

'Mostly afternoons and evenings.'

'Do you know the people?' said Willi.

'No, I don't know them,' said Fritz. 'I don't know what they're doing back there.'

'I wonder whether it's some kind of scientific laboratory,' said Willi. 'Does that sound right?'

'Hmm,' said Fritz. 'Do you think it's drugs? God, I hope not.'

'I don't know,' said Willi.

Fritz opened a drawer in his desk and pulled out a jar and schnapps glass. He unscrewed the lid, poured himself a full glass, and drank it down. 'How about a schnapps, Wilhelm?' he said.

'Sure, Fritz. Thanks.'

Fritz filled the glass again and Willi drank it down. His throat caught fire, he coughed, his eyes watered.

Fritz laughed. 'Good stuff, huh, Wilhelm?'

'Excellent,' said Willi. His voice caught, and Fritz laughed again. 'By the way, Fritz,' said Willi once his voice came back, 'can you see the place from back there?' He pointed toward the back of the warehouse.

'Come with me,' said Fritz. There were no customers, and he was happy for the diversion. Willi followed him back between the stacks of lumber and racks of trim to a small window that looked out on to the courtyard.

The building across from them, number nine, the wine merchant, had an old double door that opened onto the courtyard. 'That's how they got the wine barrels in and out,' said Fritz. 'And there's the entrance to the place you're looking at.'

Three broad steps led up to a tall, narrow wooden door. The door looked rickety enough, but there was a large new padlock in place. Above the door and to the left were clerestory windows.

'You don't have a way into the courtyard from here, do you?' said Willi. 'I'm thinking they wouldn't have built a building like this without a door of some kind . . .'

'No,' said Fritz. 'I can't help you there.'

'Because,' said Willi, 'it would be a big help, Fritz, if I could just get in there and get a feel for the place. I'll be renting the courtyard too, and I need to see it without the city tax people looking over my shoulder.'

'Like I said . . .'

'I'd never tell anyone, Fritz. And I'd be grateful, it would be a big favor. You could save me some real time and money . . .'

Fritz studied Willi for a moment. He brushed his mustache rapidly with a forefinger. 'OK, Wilhelm,' he said finally. 'But you've got to be quick, and you can't tell a soul.'

'I promise, Fritz,' said Willi. 'No one will ever know.'

Just a few steps further toward the back of the warehouse was a rack of parquet. 'Give me a hand,' said Fritz. The two of them pulled the rack away from the wall and a small door came into view. Fritz unlatched and opened it. 'Hurry up, Wilhelm. You can't ever say a word to anyone. I'd lose my job.'

Willi slipped through the opening and into the courtyard. He hurried up the three steps to get a closer look at the padlock. It was a Krax. He thought one of the keys on Ottmar's key ring had been a Krax. He looked at the spaces around the door for a key, but there was none to be seen. Then he trotted across to the double door to have a look, and then back and slipped through the door back into the warehouse. Fritz was waiting nervously, and together they slid the rack of parquet back into place.

Fritz took another drink of schnapps to calm his nerves. He held the jar and the glass out for Willi.

'No, thanks,' said Willi.

'You can't say a word, Wilhelm,' said Fritz again.

'I promise,' said Willi again. 'I really appreciate it. In fact, Fritz, let me buy you a beer and an Albertus when you get off work.'

Fritz's eyes lit up. Albertus was the champagne of brandies. 'I get off at six,' he said.

Willi was back at six. Fritz locked the door, looked up and down the street to be sure no one else was watching, and slid the large iron key into a crack between the stones above the door.

THE KEY

The desk sergeant kept a tall, narrow filing cabinet in his office. Its drawers were full of keys organized alphabetically by manufacturer. Early in his career, Ludwig Voss had had the idea that a collection of keys could be useful and had put one together over the last thirty years. On the day of his retirement, he gave the cabinet to the precinct. Eventually the department ordered it destroyed. You could see why.

But for now Willi was able to sign out the handful of Krax keys, including one that looked like a skeleton.

'You forgot to put down the case you're working on, Geismeier,' said the sergeant checking the key registry.

'Sorry, Sergeant,' said Willi and wrote, Case 20-0310. 'The stolen weapons,' he said.

'Right,' said the sergeant.

Willi went straight home, fed Puck, had supper, and was asleep by nine.

When he wheeled his bicycle out onto the street at three thirty in the morning, not a soul was stirring. Fluffy clouds swept across the crescent moon high in the sky. The light breeze was at his back. It was a quick twenty-minute ride to Stettnerstraße 13. He took the key from the crack above the door, let himself in, went through the lumberyard, out the back door, and across the courtyard. The sixth key he tried opened the Krax.

He went inside, closed the door, and turned on his electric torch. Shadows danced on the walls as he looked here and there. He went to the filing cabinet and opened one drawer after another – they contained notebooks, medical journals – until he came to a series of numbered folders. There were twenty-one in all – a small number, he thought, for patient files. Doctor Trevelius had hundreds of patients and had one complete wall of cabinets full of files. Willi guessed that the five-digit numbers on the folders referred to inmates. Inside one – 59033 – was a list of dates and times with other numbers, symbols and entries he would study later. He laid the file aside. Then he wrote down all the file numbers and closed the drawer.

There was laboratory equipment on the counter, some of which he recognized by sight, including scales, a centrifuge, a small bellows, a sphygmomanometer, a microscope, a spectroscope, Bunsen burners, hot plates, a bottle of gas. The cabinets contained an assortment of bottles, vials, pipettes, pipette stands, aspirators, flasks, all clean and ready for use and arranged by size. Another cabinet had filtering mediums, funnels, jars, beakers, trays. Another cabinet had jars of saline solution, formaldehyde, paraffin, mauveine, and other solutions, stains, or dyes, all neatly labeled. Willi recognized some of the names of the ordinary chemicals that had gone missing, as well as jars labeled cocaine, morphine, opium.

A small white chest had two drawers full of syringes and hypodermic needles. Other drawers contained scalpels, small saws, forceps, tweezers, clamps, and other metal instruments that Willi did not recognize. A refrigerator held two trays of vials with brownish blood samples, glass slides with smears of various colors, and tiny jars with what looked like slivers of blackened lemon peel. Everything was labeled with five-digit numbers. Willi searched for and found one of the small jars with the same number as the file – 59033.

He looked at his watch. Six o'clock. He had been there over an hour. The sky was lightening. He took the file and the small jar, left the laboratory, locked the Krax, ran across the courtyard, and slipped into the lumberyard. He was pushing the rack of parquet into place, when he heard the front door open and two men arguing.

One – Willi recognized Fritz's voice – said, 'I swear I locked it, Hermann.'

'Then where's the goddamn key?'

'I swear,' said Fritz again.

The other voice – Hermann – said, 'Goddamn it, Fritz. You were probably too drunk to know what you were doing.'

'I locked it, goddamn it,' said Fritz.

'Then where's the goddamn key?'

'Isn't it obvious? Somebody found it and came in,' said Fritz.

'Well, goddamn it, Fritz. OK, let's go see what they stole.'

As they walked toward the back of the store, looking left and right at the bins and racks, Willi made his way down a different aisle toward the front. He slipped through the door just as they turned and started coming back.

'Who's that?' said Fritz, hurrying to the front.

'It's me, Fritz. Wilhelm Meier,' said Willi, stepping back inside. 'I just came by to see if you found an envelope. With my name on it. I had it yesterday, and now I can't find it. I've been worried sick. I was here yesterday,' he said, turning toward Hermann. 'I thought maybe I dropped it here.'

'We had a break-in last night,' said Fritz.

'Really? I'm sorry to hear that,' said Willi. 'Did they take anything?'

'It doesn't look like it,' said Fritz.

'We'll have to check against our inventory list,' said Hermann, still eyeing Willi.

'Did you find an envelope with Wilhelm Meier on it?' said Willi. 'It's kind of important. I couldn't sleep all night thinking about it.'

'What's that under your arm?' said Hermann.

'No, that's something else,' said Willi. 'So you didn't find anything?'

'No. I'm sorry,' said Fritz.

'OK. I'll go check at the Gasthaus,' said Willi. 'I hope it's there.'

The two men watched him ride off then stop suddenly. He got off his bicycle, stooped down, and came riding back. 'Is this your key?' said Willi, holding it up.

They watched him ride off again. 'It's six in the morning,' said Hermann. 'What's he doing here at this hour?'

'He lost something important,' said Fritz. 'You heard him. He couldn't sleep from worrying.'

'You're so gullible, Wilhelm. No, I'm telling you, that guy is up to something.'

INMATE 59033

The file folder Willi had taken contained handwritten pages titled 'Clinical History.' At the top of the first page was the patient's date of birth, the date and time of the physical examination, a specimen number which was 59033, the same as the inmate number.

Next came a list of abbreviations down the left side of the page and on to the next. Alongside every category was a numeric value and/or a verbal abbreviation. TEMP was labeled '37,' and 'N' for normal, and was obviously the patient's body temperature. P was probably pulse: '74,' 'normal.'

Willi went to Doctor Trevelius for help deciphering the rest of the list. Trevelius went down the page and on to the second. He explained that BP stood for blood pressure which was measured using a sphygmomanometer and which was considered by some to be a useful diagnostic tool for heart and brain health. '150/100/normal.' The instrument used millimeters of mercury to arrive at the two numbers. The first number, he explained, was the pressure during the heartbeat, the second number was between heartbeats. 'I don't put much stock in it,' he said. 'I think palpation is a more reliable diagnostic tool.'

PLR was pupillary light reflex, KR, CR, JR, AR were knee, chest, jaw and ankle reflex. Hematology was a new discipline, and Ottmar had drawn blood and studied it through a microscope. The patient's red and white blood cells had been counted and evaluated according to shape, size, and relative frequency.

Here the patient had been found wanting. Von Fischer had counted the blood – WBC, RBC, HBT, HCT, platelet, etc., had noted the figures, and had his own system of evaluation to each category, rating them either J or A.

'I'm sorry, Willi. I can't make out what that all means,' said Trevelius.

'Turn the page,' said Willi.

Trevelius turned the page and read:

Observations and Diagnosis

Patient 59033. A circumcised male of medium stature and weight, approximately forty years of age, sentenced to ten years for armed robbery. The patient exhibits various manifestations of degeneracy in line with his Hebraic origins.

Mental manifestations – criminality, slovenliness, fearfulness, scheming, ingratiating behavior. Dullness, cowardice. Lacks the manly virtues.

Physical manifestations – hirsute body, recessive forehead, recessive chin, stooped posture, rotten teeth, nasal deformation, poor eyesight, underdeveloped pectoral region, enlarged and deformed genitalia, Jewish flesh, Jewish blood.

'My God,' said Trevelius.

'Yes,' said Willi.

'I've never seen anything like this,' said Trevelius.

'You mean, the racialism?' said Willi.

'Yes, that, certainly that. But this reads more like the record of an experiment than like an actual clinical history of a case involving a human being. There's no diagnosis, not even a speculative one. There's no record of any history taking. None. No – "the patient complained of;" no – "the patient exhibited this or that symptom;" no – "the patient was having difficulty breathing." There's not a word from the patient. He's completely silent. Not even his name. It's like he's describing an insect or a laboratory animal.'

Willi took the little jar from his pocket. 'What do you think this is?' said Willi.

Trevelius turned the jar around a few times, stepped over to the lamp, opened the jar, held it under the lamp. 'Let me be sure,' he said. He stepped to his microscope, used a tweezer to place the sample, pushed his glasses back on his head, and peered through the microscope.

'It's human flesh,' he said.

THE WARDEN AGAIN

Warden Dunziger wasn't exactly glad to hear from Willi again, but he wasn't exactly unhappy either. After all, the detective had alerted him to some shenanigans going on among the guards. The warden had immediately dealt with the situation by calling both Ammer and Bäder to his office. They stood at attention while he berated them. He accused them both of having taken part in a serious cover-up and, in so doing, perpetrating what he called a criminal deception.

In the interest of fairness, he allowed each man to speak in his defense. Each one insisted he had had nothing to do with it, which was of course true. But the warden, even as he suspected they were telling the truth, felt that he had to put a stop to whatever it was that was going on before it went any further. Besides, Ammer's demeanor had been slovenly and disrespectful when the warden had arrived at C-8, and Bäder had come back from 'calming down' the unruly inmate with skinned knuckles and a shirt wet with perspiration. The warden decided both men should be terminated.

Ammer, who was only a few months short of retirement, began to weep. 'What about my pension, Warden, sir? It's all I have?' Bäder just glared at the floor. But that was that, and the two men were escorted to their lockers to collect their belongings and then escorted from the building.

The warden felt he had to be severe. He was already getting heat because of all the deaths from the *Spanische Grippe* among the prison population. He insisted to the mayor that was a situation of *force majeure,* something completely beyond his control. 'But that didn't keep the mayor from calling for my head. He's a socialist, you know. So you see, Herr Detective, I am under a great deal of pressure. This is not a job for the faint of heart.'

Willi told the warden that neither Ammer nor Bäder had been part of the deception. The man who had called himself Ammer might not even be a guard.

'That's impossible,' said the warden. 'But be that as it may, Detective, the situation has been dealt with.' He was sorry he had agreed to see the detective.

Willi handed the warden a paper with twenty-one five-digit numbers on it. 'I need the names of these prisoners,' said Willi, 'and their addresses, and their whereabouts – if they are deceased, still in the prison population, or have been released.'

'I have already told you, Detective, I cannot give you that information.'

'If you like, Herr Dunziger, I can return with a court order. Of course, in order to request the order, I will have to describe the Ammer-Bäder situation to the judge, since that is the justification for my request.'

'Why are you even investigating the guard situation? I told you I have dealt with it.'

'You have not deal with it, Herr Dunziger; you have tried to bury it,' said Willi. 'It is part of a larger criminal investigation. If you resist getting me the information, then you become part of the criminal enterprise.'

'That is outrageous. How dare you!' said Dunziger, turning red in the face. He crumpled up the list of numbers and threw it on the floor.

'Withholding this information, Herr Dunziger, would be obstruction of justice,' said Willi. He stooped down, picked up the crumpled list, smoothed it out, and handed it to the warden.

Dunziger pretended to study the list of numbers, fighting to calm himself as he did. Finally he said, 'All right. I'll have the information for you tomorrow.'

'I need it now. I'll give you an hour.'

Willi waited in the outer office. The warden returned after forty-five minutes with several sheets of paper. Willi glanced at the pages, folded them, and put them in his jacket pocket. 'Thank you for your cooperation, Warden Dunziger.' He held out his hand. The warden had little choice but to take it.

A SURPRISE

Werner Heisse, Willi's first partner from the days in Sergeant Schobert's old squad, had been in the trenches for all four years of the war. He was a ferocious fighter, which would have surprised no one. He was wounded four different times, and each time was more eager than before to get back to the action.

He was promoted to corporal then to sergeant, and might have been made an officer if the times and circumstances had allowed it. But he was not 'officer material,' as the other officers said

– not evaluating his military prowess, which was prodigious, so much as his place on the social register. When the war ended, he went home with a chest full of medals, including two iron crosses, first and second class.

But Werner was not suited for the peace. The politics were shit, the people were shit, the country was shit. He tried to rejoin the police force, but they wouldn't have him. Anyway, he said, the police were shit too. The only thing the war had prepared him for was a life of villainy. So he lived by stealing – breaking and entering, sticking people up. He did it the way he fought – impulsively, recklessly – and was eventually caught, tried, and sent to Stadelheim for thirty months. After four years in the trenches, he could do thirty months standing on his head.

There were twenty-one names and numbers on Willi's list. The first twelve were deceased, the next seven were alive and still incarcerated, and the last two had been released: Karl Schmidt, two weeks earlier, and Werner Heisse (number 52701), just ten days ago. There was no address for Karl Schmidt but Werner Heisse lived at 420 Landsbergerstraße.

Number 420 was a decrepit tenement house among small warehouses, cut-rate shops, and other tenements all jammed together up against a pair of railroad trunk lines five kilometers west of Munich's central station. The railroad was under constant repair or construction, so when trains weren't running there was still constant noise and smoke and the smell of machinery at work. Werner's shack looked uninhabitable from the street, although a stovepipe poking through the nearly flat roof and held in place by cables was smoking.

Willi knocked at the door and waited. He knocked again, and then again. The door was finally opened by a woman who, Willi guessed, was younger than she looked. 'What?' she said.

'I'm looking for Werner Heisse,' said Willi.

'He's not here,' she said.

'When do you expect him back?' said Willi.

'How should I know?' she said, and started to close the door.

'Tell him that Willi Geismeier stopped by,' said Willi.

'Geismeier!' Werner shouted from somewhere inside. 'Let him in, Ilse.'

Ilse stepped aside and Willi stepped inside. 'In there,' she said, and pointed to a doorway at the end of a short hall.

Werner Heisse struggled to stand up from the broken-down chair where he spent his days. 'Give me your hand, Geismeier,' he said, and finally managed to wobble to his feet. He grinned at Willi and pumped his hand. He was missing teeth. 'Goddamn, man. You're still a goddamn cop, aren't you? I can see it just looking at you.' He laughed and his laugh turned into a cough that wouldn't stop.

He lowered himself back on to the chair. The room was tiny, contained the chair, a small table, some shelves with knickknacks and a small coal-burning stove that was going full tilt and leaking smoke into the room. The floor sagged, the walls were hung with old carpets and curtains to keep out the cold. The little house shook as a train roared by.

A gray and white cat wandered into the room and jumped on Werner's lap. Werner threw up his hands like something unexpected had landed on him. 'Goddamn beast,' he said. 'I don't like them, but Ilse does. So.'

He stroked the cat which started to purr.

'I'm glad to see you, Werner,' said Willi.

'I just got out of the joint, Geismeier, but I guess you know that, you smart bastard.' Werner laughed again, this time without the cough. 'You know, when I was doing shit, I stayed out of your precinct, because I was sure if I got anywhere nearby, you'd catch me sure as hell. Well, somebody caught me anyway. Turns out I wasn't very good at serious crime.'

'Are you ill, Werner?' said Willi.

'Oh, I'm all right, Willi. It's just that life has taken its toll on me.'

'Are you seeing a doctor?' said Willi.

'You know, Schobert told me you're in his squad now. Don't tell him I told you; he'd be pissed off. He helps me out a little from time to time. My army pension amounts to pennies, you know, Willi.'

'I didn't know,' said Willi. He took out his billfold. 'Here, Werner.'

'Thanks, Geismeier. Really, I mean it. Thanks a lot.'

'Have you been sick for a long time, Werner?'

'No. I was in pretty good shape until the *Spanische Grippe* found me. It knocked the shit out of me.'

'While you were in prison, you mean?' said Willi.

'Yeah,' said Werner. 'I got vaccinated, you know. But I guess it was already in me, the sickness, I mean.'

'Who vaccinated you, Werner?' said Willi.

Werner put his hand to his chest. 'I don't like to dwell on it, Willi. Let's talk about something else. Remember how we solved old Metzger's murder? That newspaperman that killed him? You thought it was me for a while, didn't you?'

'No, Werner. I honestly didn't. Killing wasn't your style.'

'You were always such a smartass, Willi. I remember how you used to piss me off. But the way you came at shit sideways, Willi, that was something to behold. Believe it or not, I learned a lot from you. Looking at shit sideways.'

'Werner, I've got a doctor friend. His name is Trevelius. I'd like you to let him have a look at you. He's smart, and maybe he could do something for you.'

'No need, Willi. Really. I've got a first-rate doctor looking after me.'

'You do? That's good to hear.'

'You know the one good thing about Stadelheim? First they got me vaccinated, then when the *Grippe* found me, they treated me. And then, when I got out, they continued to treat me. Now you tell me, Willi, who gets that kind of medical care?'

'You mean Doctor von Fischer?' said Willi.

'That's him, Doctor Ottmar von Fischer.'

'And he's still looking after you, is he?'

'He is. He says he's gonna get me back on my feet again, and I believe him.'

'Where does he treat you?' said Willi.

'He comes here,' said Werner.

'How often does he come?' said Willi.

'Every four days,' he said with a laugh. 'I've got the scars to prove it.' Werner pulled up a shirt sleeve. His arm was bruised purple and yellow. There were a dozen black spots where he had been injected. Then he pulled up the other sleeve and revealed a dozen more.

SCHOBERT

'Sergeant Schobert?' said Willi. 'Could I have a word?'

'All right, Geismeier, come in.'

'It's about Werner Heisse, Sergeant.'

'Werner Heisse? What about him?'

'Well, first of all I've been to see him.'

'You have? And why is that, Geismeier?'

'Because I came across his name in the course of my investigation.'

'The stolen weapons? He's got nothing to do with that. The man can hardly stand, and he was in prison until a few days ago.'

'Not the stolen weapons, Sergeant.'

'What then?'

'It's an offshoot of the drug case. It involves Doctor Ottmar von—'

'*What?*' Schobert jumped up. 'Goddamn you, Geismeier! You just can't follow orders, can you! You were told to stay away from the doctors, the hospital, the drugs, especially *that* doctor. You've finally gone too far, Geismeier. Your ass is finished.'

'Sergeant, I have evidence that Werner Heisse is being systematically poisoned by Doctor Ottmar von Fischer, and Werner is just one of at least twenty-one people who have been poisoned by Fischer and perhaps are still being poisoned by him. Twelve have died, so far.'

Schobert stared at Willi with his jaw hanging open. 'Are you goddamn crazy? Jesus Christ! You've really gone around the bend this time, Geismeier. OK, I'm removing you from duty, effective immediately.' He held out his hand. 'Give me your badge and gun.'

'First, listen to the evidence, Sergeant. Then, if you still want me to, I'll turn in my badge and gun, and you'll never see me again. But just listen to what I've got.'

'Geismeier, you've acted against instructions, went behind my back, conducted a completely unauthorized investigation, and now you're accusing a public hero of mass murder . . .'

'Just listen to what I have, Sergeant.'

Sergeant Schobert did not like Detective Willi Geismeier. He had *never* liked the son of a bitch, not from the first day he had laid eyes on him. He was a spoiled rich kid. First in his goddamn class. He was always bending the rules, flouting procedures, going against authority, like it was some goddamn game – and now this.

OK, it was true, Geismeier *had* solved some big cases, and, yes, his case closure rate was the best in the whole goddamn district. He had good – all right, amazing – instincts. And, he didn't make shit up. Schobert took out his watch and laid it on the desk in front of him. 'You've got ten minutes,' he said.

He figured, *OK, I'll hear him out. Ten minutes listening to this crazy bullshit, and then I'm free to get rid of him forever.* But as Willi told him about the death of the two Gabeks, the fake prison guards, the fake vaccines, the almost impossible coincidence that only prisoners had gotten sick – even Schobert had wondered about that – Fischer's interest in eugenics, the secret Stettnerstraße lab, and Werner's worsening condition – 'have you seen his arms, Sergeant? He's been stuck dozens of times' – Schobert realized that Geismeier wasn't completely nuts, that maybe there was mass murder going on right under their noses. It at least warranted an official investigation.

Then Schobert realized that if he authorized such an investigation it would involve search warrants, interviews with people in high places, stepping on lots of toes. Fischer was widely respected, was politically connected. In fact, Captain Reineke was an admirer, and so were lots of other higher-ups. Jesus. It wouldn't be just Geismeier whose career would be over.

Willi continued. 'There are living prisoners who didn't die from Fischer's treatments we can interview. I've got a list of names. And Werner can certainly shed more light on the case. Von Fischer has records in his lab, and I'm sure he has others hidden somewhere.'

By the time Schobert looked at his watch again, a half-hour had passed. 'OK, Geismeier, stop for a minute.'

Willi didn't stop. 'Werner is still being treated by Fischer, and—'

'*Stop!*' screamed Schobert. 'I said, stop. OK? OK. You have lots of stuff here, a lot of it, maybe most, is circumstantial, but it sounds like a case. I'll admit that, all right? You've got to give me a little time to figure out what to do.'

'A search warrant . . .'

'Will you shut the hell up, Geismeier? Jesus! Do you know *anything* about Captain Reineke?'

'I know he's got more clout than an ordinary detective captain,' said Willi.

'You've got that right, Geismeier. And if we go ahead with any of this, we'll both be finished. I'm not sure why, but the higher-ups love this Doctor von Fischer.'

'It's the race stuff, Sergeant.'

'The race stuff?' said Schobert.

'Fischer's doing crazy experiments on prisoners to prove scientifically that Jews, dark-skinned people, poor people, criminals are all racially inferior.'

'Werner's not a Jew,' said Schobert.

'But he's a criminal. Fischer believes criminals are born criminals, and should be eliminated. That's what he's trying to prove.'

'I need time to think about this, Geismeier,' said Schobert.

'We've got three days, Sergeant,' said Willi.

'What do you mean?' said Schobert.

'Werner's next treatment is in three days.'

THIN ICE

Willi had taken a chance showing Schobert his cards. But what else did he have? He needed to talk to at least some of Fischer's eight other living victims. A search revealed that Karl Schmidt, the other parolee, had disappeared. And without a court order, the warden wasn't going to let Willi anywhere near the seven inmates who presumably were still being injected. Willi also needed to get the files from Stettnerstraße and wherever else they might be. But he'd need a court order to get that done too.

Then there was Erzberger. Willi was sure Erzberger was responsible for the stolen drugs. He would also know about the concoctions Fischer was shooting into people's arms. But Erzberger was even better connected than Fischer, so again, interrogating him without a court order was out of the question. And now what about Schobert? After thinking things over, Schobert would realize all he had to do was alert Reineke, and let Reineke lower the hammer on Willi. Then Schobert would be free of Willi *and* in Reineke's good graces. Willi worried that he had miscalculated. Badly.

Benno had been pushed out. Then Ove had been fired. A postcard had arrived from Aurich, a small town on the North Sea coast. It had a picture of women wearing long skirts, using wooden farm implements to rake and stack hay. On the other side was a note in Ove's squarish hand: *Determination, Willi. You're on the right track. O.S.*

Even Ludwig had finally put in his papers. He'd often said he was going to do it, and now he finally had. Willi had ventured alone onto thin ice, and he feared the ice was giving way.

Izabella Bauer did not seem surprised to hear from Willi. She said she had time after work and suggested they meet at the place where they had met for coffee earlier. It was six o'clock. There were no customers. The waiter was behind the bar polishing glasses. Willi and Izabella shook hands. 'Sit wherever you like,' said the waiter. They sat at the table where they had sat before. The waiter brought menus.

'Just a beer for me,' said Willi.

'I'll have one too,' said Izabella.

'Did Gregor Wertheimer get any reaction after he asked about Gabek?' said Willi.

'No,' said Izabella. 'Neither did I. What about you?'

'I did,' said Willi. 'Wertheimer shook things up.'

'In what way?' said Izabella.

'It's an ongoing investigation,' said Willi. 'I can't say much. Is Wertheimer going to keep looking into the case?'

Izabella scowled at Willi. 'What case? You're asking for something, Willi, and giving me nothing in return. That police talk "ongoing investigation" stuff doesn't work with me.'

'OK, Izabella,' he said. 'I understand.'

'So what brought you here, Willi?'

'You did,' he said, realizing it and saying it in the same moment. 'I'm in a precarious situation, and I need . . . a friend.'

Izabella signaled the waiter. 'We're going to have supper after all. Go on,' she said, once the waiter had left.

Willi was at a loss. 'I've gotten myself in a situation . . .'

She waited, but he couldn't continue. 'About the doctor and the inmates?' she said.

He didn't answer.

The waiter came and took their order, then brought their food. They ate in silence without even knowing what they were eating.

'Your Wertheimer really shook things up,' said Willi, shaking his head.

'So you said, Willi. In what way?' said Izabella.

'OK. Well, first off, the doctor, Ottmar von Fischer, and Gerhard Erzberger, the university's head lab technician, skipped out of the reception when they heard Wertheimer's question. They made a beeline for a place on Stettnerstraße right behind the prison.'

'What's there?' said Izabella.

'A secret laboratory,' said Willi.

'Really? Can you get in?' said Izabella.

'I did,' said Willi.

'And?'

'It's von Fischer's lab. I found evidence he's experimenting on prison inmates.'

Izabella stared at him.

'And some of them are dying. Twelve have, so far.'

Izabella put both hands over her mouth. 'Mother of God,' she said. 'Mother of God.'

'I know,' said Willi.

'And he hasn't been arrested?'

'Arrested? He hasn't even been investigated. Because he's protected. I was ordered off the case. Long ago, actually.'

'How can I help?' said Izabella, and then did something neither he nor she expected. She took his hand in both of hers and held it while he told her everything he knew.

Willi paid the bill. They left the restaurant and started walking. Izabella put her arm through his.

They walked in silence for a while, each one feeling like the earth was unsteady under their feet. They were alone in a world where the likes of Ottmar von Fischer, Erzberger, their admirers and disciples flourished, and humanity seemed to be in mortal peril.

'I have something to say,' said Izabella. They stopped walking. She withdrew her arm from his. 'I want to say this plainly.' She took a deep breath. 'I was married for two years. We lived in Berlin. My husband and our son were killed there in a freak accident a year and a half ago.'

Willi did not say 'I'm sorry,' the way most people did, and she was glad of that.

'A year and a half sounds like a long time, but it feels like yesterday. Every day it feels like yesterday. There are days where I am so lonely that I want to kill myself. I am being smothered by loneliness.'

Willi did not say anything.

'I can see that you're lonely too.'

'You can see that?' said Willi.

'I think I can,' she said.

'OK,' said Willi.

'How old are you, Willi?'

'Twenty-seven,' said Willi.

'I'm thirty-five,' she said.

'I don't care about that,' said Willi.

'So, you can tell where I'm going,' she said, and smiled.

'I'm a detective,' he said.

She laughed. 'I don't believe in love at first sight. Do you?'

Willi considered the question. 'In general or in particular?' he said.

She laughed again.

'I don't know how else to say this,' said Izabella. 'I want to end this loneliness. I want you to help me end this loneliness.'

Willi didn't say anything.

'Does that scare you?' she said.

'Yes, a little,' said Willi.

'OK. Me too this is my building,' she said.

Willi looked up at the building. 'Which floor?' he said.
'Third,' she said. 'Will you come up with me?'
'I can't,' said Willi. 'My cat needs to be fed. How about if
you come home with me? Will you come home with me?'
'Yes,' said Izabella. She took his arm, pulled him to her and
kissed him, on the mouth this time.

GREGOR WERTHEIMER

I t was a cold rainy Sunday. The windows were steamed up.
Willi slipped out of bed, dressed, went downstairs. By the time
Izabella came down, he had fed Puck again, had made coffee,
warmed some milk, and put out black bread, butter, confiture –
marmalade and raspberry – and cheese on the table.

'Good morning,' she said. Her hair was going every which
way.

'Good morning,' said Willi. She liked his smile. It seemed
confident without taking anything for granted. They hugged each
other. Each one thought: *So this is how it feels. I remember this
feeling. A loving body is a safe harbor in a stormy sea.*

The black bread was fresh from the bakery. Willi cut off thick
slabs. The marmalade was sweet and bitter, the raspberry was
more fruit than jam, the butter soft and fat and sweet. It was the
happiest, best meal they could remember. They didn't say much
while they ate.

'What are your plans for today?' said Willi.

'I'll go into the paper,' said Izabella. 'Sunday's a workday for
me.' She paused. 'I've been thinking,' she said. 'You should come
meet Gregor Wertheimer.'

'Because?' said Willi.

'There's a story to be told about people who survived the
Grippe – both victims and their families – how they did it, how
they're doing. A human-interest feature story. I can give him the
names of the surviving inmates without ever mentioning von
Fischer or the case or anything about it. Gregor is an enterprising
reporter – he'll find the families, ask them about their inmate

relatives. It would be surprising, wouldn't it, if something didn't turn up? What do you think?'

'I shouldn't meet him,' said Willi.

'You don't want me to do it?' said Izabella.

'I wouldn't say that,' said Willi. 'I just shouldn't be part of it.'

Izabella described the idea. Gregor didn't like it. 'You're talking about a feature story. I'm a reporter,' he said. 'Give it to Detlev.' Detlev Franzen was a society reporter. He covered galas and horse shows, that sort of thing.

'I'd like you to do it, Gregor,' said Izabella, handing him the list of names.

'Why?' said Gregor.

'Because I think it's more than a feature,' said Izabella.

'Shit,' said Gregor. 'Maybe I'll go see if they can make better use of my talents at *Die Presse.*'

'Maybe you should,' said Izabella.

Gregor had made the same threat at least three times in the last six months. It was on the verge of becoming a standing joke in the newsroom.

Once he had calmed down, he worked his way down the list of inmates, searching police records, city directories to find their homes and families. Most lived in impoverished conditions, and most were ignorant of the treatment their relative was receiving, since the inmates were quarantined and visits had been cancelled.

A few had received letters from husbands or fathers indicating the treatments continued. Some were improving, some were not. A Frau Schickel told him that her husband, in prison for robbery, claimed that he had been vaccinated by his doctor, even though she, who had been a nurse in the war, was pretty sure that couldn't be true. 'I told him there's no vaccine for the *Spanische Grippe.* I'm right, aren't I?' she said.

'I'll look into it,' said Gregor.

A week after Izabella had given Gregor the assignment, she saw him at his desk. He was leafing through his notes before going out for another interview. 'How's it going, Gregor? When are you going to have something for me?'

'This is a bigger story than you imagined,' he said. 'I need more time.'

'Really?'

'There's something else here,' he said.

'Maybe you'd like to take it over to *Die Presse* where they'd value your talent.' She couldn't resist.

'Screw you,' said Gregor.

SCHOBERT

The Monday morning after their meeting, Schobert called Willi back into his office. 'Werner's safe,' he said.

'What do you mean, safe?' said Willi.

'He's in a safe place. When the doctor shows up at his place tomorrow, he won't be there.'

'Where is he?' said Willi.

'Someplace safe.'

'How'd you persuade him to go?' said Willi.

'I suggested a break from his treatments would be a good idea.'

'What did you tell him about von Fischer?'

'Nothing. I just said some fresh air might be a good change.'

'OK,' said Willi. 'And what's happening with von Fischer?'

'Nothing,' said Schobert. 'For now. Meanwhile you should continue to gather evidence if you can.'

'Can I get a court order to search the lab?'

'No. No court order. And don't even think of going behind my back. I'll know it if you do, and that'll be the last thing you ever do as a policeman, I promise you.'

Willi guessed that Schobert had told Reineke about what he was up to. From now on, they would try to short-circuit his investigation.

Willi guessed right. Schobert had gone to Reineke's apartment building the evening before, thinking Reineke would rather have this discussion in private. Reineke was not happy to see Sergeant Schobert on a Sunday evening. 'What do you want, Schobert?'

Schobert said he had compelling and urgent evidence that Doctor Ottmar von Fischer, the university doctor who served as the prison doctor, was doing experiments on living prison inmates, and some of them had died.

Reineke looked up and down the hall, 'Come inside, Sergeant,' said Reineke. He led Schobert down a narrow hall. They passed a closed door where Schobert heard the murmuring of men's voices.

'A card game,' said Reineke. They reached a small study and Reineke remained standing. He turned to face Schobert. 'Now, regarding von Fischer's experiments – and I tell you this in the strictest confidence – as I understand it, Schobert, he is working on some new and innovative treatments for the *Spanische Grippe*, and he has been trying out these treatments on prisoners who have fallen ill with the disease and have no other hope.'

'Yes, Captain, but there is some indication, Captain, I don't quite know how to say this, sir, but the prisoners were . . . that is . . . they may have been infected by von Fischer himself.'

'What the devil are you saying, Schobert?'

'That the doctor injected them with the disease himself, Captain.'

'That is an outrageous accusation, Sergeant Schobert. Where the devil does this come from?'

'It comes from Detective Geismeier, Captain.'

'I might have known,' said Reineke, rolling his eyes in disgust.

'Yes, Captain. Although I have to say, with all respect, Captain, he has evidence to support it.'

'Schobert,' said Reineke. He took a step closer to Schobert. 'Schobert,' he said again and poked his finger against the sergeant's chest, 'I strongly suggest you not repeat this renegade detective's wild imaginings, if you know what's good for you. Even if it were true that prisoners had died, would it really be so terrible if a couple of miscreants and Jews were to give their lives for the advancement of science?'

'Jews?' said Schobert.

'That's what I'm told,' said Reineke.

'So you know about this, Captain?' said Schobert.

'Is there a problem, Sergeant?' said Reineke. 'Doctor von Fischer is a ground-breaking scientist. His ways are unconventional, true, but he is on the verge of important scientific advances.

He is pushing the limits of eugenic biology. The path to a master race is not going to be a walk in the park. No, the only problem I see facing you, is how you're going to control that goddamn Geismeier.'

Willi had reached the limits of what he could accomplish on his own. His investigation was about to stall. If he pushed any further, he could come up against Reineke and the whole German/racialist movement that was rising like a tsunami. Schobert could protect Werner, and he would. As for all the rest, that was somebody else's business.

FRESH AIR

Werner's sister Irena had one of those public garden allotments that residents could claim along the railroad tracks. She had had it for years, and had built a little hut. Vines had grown up over it. She had a peach, an apple, and a cherry tree out front. Inside were her gardening supplies and a little cot where she could rest.

The bus that went out there from the city stopped on Landsbergerstraße near Werner's house, so it was an easy thirty-minute ride for Werner. The plan was he would go there each morning and then take the streetcar back each night. He was too sick to do much of anything besides sit around anyway.

It wasn't much of a hiding place. Willi found Werner dozing on a rickety bench in front of the hut. His breathing was labored. Willi sat down beside him and Werner woke up.

'Schobert thought you'd be safe here,' said Willi.

Werner rolled his eyes. 'Don't be ridiculous,' he said.

'Did he tell you why he thought you should leave?' said Willi.

'No,' said Werner. 'He said the country air would do me good. He said a break from the treatment would do me good.' He waved his arm in the direction of the railroad tracks no more than a hundred meters away. 'Country air, my ass.'

'Listen, Werner . . .' said Willi.

'No, *you* listen, Geismeier. All of a sudden you show up out of the blue after how many years. All you want to talk about is my vaccination, my medical treatment, my doctor. Then you want me to switch to your doctor, then Schobert sends me out here. So, something's going on. I'm guessing something's screwy with Fischer. So suppose you stop treating me like an idiot and tell me what's going on.'

'OK, Werner, fair enough. Your vaccination, was it in your arm?' said Willi.

'No. My chest,' said Werner. 'It looked like a needle for a horse. It hurt like a son of a bitch.'

'Show me where,' said Willi.

Werner opened his shirt. His chest was shrunken, white and boney. He pointed at a black spot just below his heart.

'No matter what Fischer says, there's no vaccination for the *Spanische Grippe*.'

'So, what was it, then?' said Werner.

'I think he was injecting you with the disease. I think he was trying to infect you with the disease.'

Werner thought about it for a long minute. 'Jesus. So, you're saying the bastard makes me sick, me and the other cons – because you know there are a bunch of us got sick around the same time – so he can try out his remedies on us, which is why he's injecting stuff into my arm every four or five days? And then he takes blood and goes back to his laboratory, right? And looks at it through his microscope so he can plan the next shit he's going to stick me with, is that right?'

'That's pretty much it, Werner. Remedies, maybe. I don't know at this point.'

'What do you mean?' said Werner.

'He may be injecting you with other stuff that has nothing to do with the *Grippe* or even anything medical.'

'What do you mean?' said Werner again.

'Maybe he's just doing what he calls experiments.'

'Jesus. Why would the sick bastard do this shit?' said Werner.

'Eugenics,' said Willi.

'What's that?' said Werner.

'He thinks criminals, like you, are inferior beings,' said Willi.

'I'm not a criminal. I was one, but I'm not any more,' said Werner.

'Well, he believes you were born that way. You have no choice; you're still a criminal, because you were born a criminal. Same with poor people, black and brown people, Jews, the feeble-minded; in fact, everybody, except those he calls "Germans." And since you and all these other people are sub-humans, doing experiments on them – and you – is just no big deal.'

Werner took a minute to let all this sink in. Then he said, 'To hell with him. I'm going home.'

'What are you going to do?' said Willi.

'Just going home,' said Werner. 'I don't like being away from Ilse. And she won't leave that damned cat.'

'All right,' said Willi.

'And what are you going to do?' said Werner.

'I'm working on it,' said Willi.

'But Schobert's standing in your way, isn't he?' said Werner.

'Well, he's certainly not helping,' said Willi, 'but . . .'

'You'll find a way, Geismeier,' said Werner with a laugh. 'You sly bastard, you always do, don't you?'

'We'll see,' said Willi. 'What are you going to do when Fischer comes for his next appointment? When is that?'

'Wednesday. Day after tomorrow,' said Werner. 'He's not getting in the door.'

'You're not going to try anything . . .?' said Willi.

'Look at me, Willi. I can hardly stand up. What could I possibly do?'

TUESDAY

Doctor von Fischer was going to be performing surgery on a patient with a ruptured appendix at eight in the morning, and Willi was eager to attend. He had asked Peter Strauß to sign him up. He was of course interested in seeing von Fischer's psychopathology on display, and wondered whether it would be as plain to see as Doctor Albertsohn had suggested. But more importantly, he wondered who else might show up once Ottmar saw Detective Willi Geismeier on the registry list.

Willi decided he would wear his uniform so he would be easy to spot.

Willi arrived at seven forty-five. The theater was a circular arena with six levels of seats ascending the steep sides. The seats were filling up with doctors wearing white coats, and students wearing their customary black suits and ties. What conversation there was hushed. They looked Willi up and down as he took his place three rows up by one of the stairways.

At about five minutes before eight, the patient – a young woman with a light towel over her eyes and sheets over her body – was wheeled through the door from the adjacent clinic, followed by four masked doctors wearing white gowns and rubber gloves. One, the anesthesiologist, a surgical student, began administering the ether. With one hand he held a mask of metal mesh covered with gauze over the patient's nose and mouth, and with the other he tipped a small bottle with a strip of gauze hanging from its mouth, allowing drops of ether to form and then fall one by one on to the gauze.

Ottmar strode into the theater, his gown flowing out behind him. Willi looked at his watch; it was precisely eight o'clock. Ottmar dipped his hands into a pitcher of phenol and alcohol and put on rubber gloves. He then addressed the audience, wishing them a good morning, thanking them for coming, speaking briefly about the value that watching a master surgeon at work had for young aspirants. Surgery, he said, was the queen of medical specialties. His eyes swept the room, and Willi thought he saw a flicker of recognition as they swept past him.

Ottmar said removing the appendix was an absolutely routine piece of surgery, even a ruptured one should pose no problem for the practiced hand. He held up his own hand for the crowd to admire. There were a few chuckles.

The appendix, he said, was a useless little tube, a worm-like appendage that can be found in various positions relative to the surrounding viscera. Most often it was retro-cecal – that is, behind the cecum, the large intestine. Or it could be, and frequently was, pelvic, so pointing toward the pelvic brim. There were other possibilities of course: pre-ileal, then post-ileal, etcetera.

'Palpation will give you a clue where it is, since the pain varies from location to location. You play the patient's belly like a musical instrument. Although once an appendix has ruptured, the patient's pain is too great and dispersed to be of much use. It is like pressing all the keys at once.' He pressed his fist into the patient's lower abdomen. But she was by now anesthetized and gave no reaction.

Ottmar picked up a scalpel and passed it back and forth lightly between his left and right hands, as though he were deciding which hand to use. 'Let's see what we have here, shall we?' He pulled the bottom sheet down and the top sheet up, exposing the white flesh of her lower belly, and made a quick motion that was more like the lunge of a swordsman than the careful cut Willi had expected – even after having heard Doctor Albertsohn's trout analogy. Her belly split open, turned red, and her viscera popped from the wound. Willi gasped involuntarily, and so did others around him. Ottmar was bent over, looking down into the wound. Willi was too far away to smell anything, but the doctors standing nearby did, and turned their heads, pulling out handkerchiefs and covering their noses.

'Too bad,' said Ottmar. 'Necrosis.'

Using various instruments, he scraped and clipped and cut, and after fifteen more minutes, nodded to one of the other surgeons who began sewing her up. Ottmar looked up at the crowd, waved his hand in the air – this time he did look directly at Willi – and left the theater.

'Did you find it illuminating, Herr Geismeier?' said Erzberger. Willi wondered whether this guy ever approached you from the front. Erzberger was accompanied by five men, four in business suits and one in the notched black collar of a priest.

'Yes, I did,' said Willi. 'My first time. Not yours I take it, Herr Erzberger.'

'No,' said Erzberger. 'But it is always illuminating to see Herr Doctor von Fischer at work.'

'Geismeier,' said Willi, and offered his hand to each of the other men, bowing his head each time as a polite German still did in those days. Four of the five, also being polite Germans, gave him their names. The priest held out a limp hand and made a weird little curtsey. He smiled, revealing a row of glittering silver teeth. Back at the station, Willi learned that the man who called himself 'Father Johannes' was Johannes Kundse, the archbishop's executive assistant.

The fifth man withheld his hand and his name. '*Detective . . .*' he said, placing heavy emphasis on the word. He was obviously a police official higher up the chain of command than Willi could ever dream of climbing. His menace was unmistakable. After a moment's thought, Willi guessed that this might be Police Chief Erich Lampe, the man who had replaced Benno von Horvath. Back at the station he learned that he had guessed correctly.

Three of the men – the police chief, the priest, and Erzberger – wore lapel pins of a sort Willi had seen for the first time only a few days earlier: a red square with a white circle and broken black cross in the middle, the symbol we now know as the swastika.

WEDNESDAY

That night Willi slept on the sofa in front of the fireplace where he could hear anybody trying to come into the house. His pistol was on the end table by his head. Puck kept watch beside him. Nobody came. In fact, Willi slept so soundly, he wondered whether he would have heard them if they had.

Willi arrived at 420 Landsbergerstraße at six thirty Wednesday morning. There was no smoke coming from the chimney, a good sign. After some negotiation, Werner had promised he would be somewhere else when von Fischer showed up for their eight thirty appointment. 'I'm not a fool,' he said.

'Someplace safe,' said Willi. 'Not your sister's garden house.'

Werner said he and Ilse and the cat of course would stay with an old friend – Pinky, he called him – who lived out in Rosenheim, sixty kilometers south-east of the city. 'Here's the address. You'll let me know when it's safe to come back.'

'What time are you leaving?' said Willi.

'Around six this evening. Come see, if you don't believe me,' said Werner.

When Willi showed up at five thirty, Werner had to laugh.

'You suspicious bastard,' he said. But there were packed bags by the door and Ilse was in the process of trying to get the cat into a small wooden carrier. There was a knock at the door. 'This is Pinky,' said Werner. Willi and Pinky shook hands. Soon the car was loaded, and then they were gone.

But with Werner you never knew, so Willi had come back in the morning to make sure. He knocked on the door. There was no response. The door was rickety, the lock was old and flimsy, and with the help of a small hooked implement, Willi let himself in. The wood stove was cold. They were gone. Willi looked around and then left.

At exactly eight thirty, Doctor von Fischer drove up and parked right in front of the house. He got out of the car carrying his small black bag. He knocked on the door. There was no answer. He knocked again. No answer. He tried the door and it was locked. He knocked again, and again, and again.

'Jesus,' said Werner, watching through the windshield of Pinky's car. 'What is it with that guy?'

Finally, Ottmar got in his car and drove off.

'OK, Pinky,' said Werner.

Pinky started the car and followed Ottmar. When they drove past the university, Pinky said, 'Where the hell's he going?'

'Just don't lose him, Pinky.'

'Sure, Werner. I know.'

Werner and Pinky had been friends since childhood, when with two other friends they had quit school and begun roaming the streets. They didn't do any hard crime, just juvenile stuff – breaking into abandoned buildings and taking whatever they could find, painting graffiti, and drinking. Once somebody found a gun, but it didn't work. Once they started a fire, but then Pinky stomped it out. Sometimes they just hung out, imagining out loud all the things they were going to do when they were men.

When they were about sixteen, they fell out, went their separate ways, and then lost track of each other altogether. Werner and Pinky hadn't seen each other for more than fifteen years when they spotted each other across the yard in Stadelheim Prison.

Pinky had spent the years before the war in Paris, where he

had gotten a job driving for a rich guy who turned out to be a bank robber. The guy wanted to train him to be a getaway driver. The first time Pinky got behind the wheel and started driving, he felt like he had been doing it all his life. 'You're a natural,' said the guy. The guy called him Pierre, and Pinky liked the sound of it and kept the name.

When the war broke out, Pinky came back to Germany to join the army and, of all the luck, was trained as a tank driver. He hated the war, but loved driving that tank. When the war ended, he had just signed up to be a pilot. 'I never met anything I couldn't drive,' he said.

'Christ, there's Stadelheim,' said Pinky. 'I don't like this.'

'Relax, Pinky,' said Werner.

Ottmar stopped the car, got out, and took his doctor's bag. He turned the corner and walked down Stettnerstraße.

'Follow him, Pinky, and when we get where he's going, I'm going to jump out.'

'You ain't doing any jumping, Werner, that's for sure,' said Pinky.

'Right, Pinky. So keep him from going inside until I can get to him.'

When Ottmar came to the courtyard gate, Pinky stopped the car and got out. 'Excuse me, sir,' he said. 'I'm looking for number nine.'

'This is number eleven,' said Ottmar. 'It must be . . .' He turned to his right and there was Werner, unsteady, hunched over in pain, and grinning.

Ottmar was confused. How could this crippled, damaged, fate-fully ill, sub-human specimen have his hands on him – like vices – and be forcing Ottmar through the gate? 'Don't wait, Pinky,' said Werner. He motioned with his head that Ottmar should step into the courtyard. 'Close the gate, Doc.'

Ottmar closed the gate. 'Now,' said Werner, holding on to the doctor's arm with one hand to hold himself upright and putting his other hand on the doctor's throat and squeezing just enough so Ottmar knew how strong he was, 'over there, up those stairs, and inside. And if you try any shit of any kind, my thumb is going straight through your windpipe and out the other side.' He gave his thumb a little push so Ottmar could tell what he meant.

Inside the laboratory, Werner said, 'Give me a tour, Doc.'

Ottmar started to talk about genetics and human development.

'I don't want to hear your shit. I just want to see where you do it.'

Ottmar was strong and fit, and it finally dawned on him that all he had to do was make a quick jump and spin around and he would break loose from Werner. And inside the black bag were several syringes and multiple doses of chemicals, any two of which would finish Werner off. He was halfway dead already.

Ottmar gave a mighty jump and Werner let go of his throat. But he still had hold of his coat, and he pulled Ottmar back toward him, and with his now free hand he swung and punched Ottmar hard in the face and broke his nose. Then, for good measure, he broke it again.

Ottmar was unfamiliar with pain. *So this is what it's like*, he thought, and went white and woozy. He sat down heavily on to a chair. When he looked up he saw Werner going through his bag.

THE AFTERMATH

T he official version of what had happened was that Herr Doctor Ottmar von Fischer had surprised a drug addict, who had broken into his laboratory looking for narcotics. The Herr Doctor had tried to calm the man down but to no avail. The man, a recently released prisoner named Werner Heisse, had assaulted the doctor, then had injected him with various chemicals he had found in the doctor's laboratory, and which, according to other doctors, had no business anywhere near the insides of a human being.

By some miracle Doctor von Fischer had survived the attack. He was in a private room in a sanatorium with police on guard around the clock. Ottmar's eyes were swollen shut. There were gauze plugs in his nose, and bandages crisscrossed his face and neck. His neck was badly torn and bruised from all the injections Werner, who had neither training nor, for that matter, interest in the proper methods for administering injections, had jabbed and poked into his neck.

Ottmar's breathing was ragged. He was mostly unconscious, although occasionally he regained consciousness and ranted incoherently, thrashing about. For that reason his arms and legs had to be tied down with ropes made of twisted gauze. Ottmar was regularly injected with various medications and calming agents. He also got hydration and nutrition through a tube inserted in his rectum. His doctors concurred that with proper care and sufficient time he would likely recover fully, but he would have to remain there for the foreseeable future.

Ottmar was visited one day by Police Chief Erich Lampe, Father Johannes Kundse, and Gerhard Erzberger. They stood at the foot of his bed while Ottmar tossed and groaned.

'Have they identified the swine that did this?' said Father Kundse.

'An animal,' said Chief Lampe. 'An ex-con named Werner Heisse. Von Fischer was his doctor.'

'Really? My God,' said Father Kundse, and crossed himself, as though he had just encountered the devil himself. 'And where is he, this . . . demon?'

'We'll get him,' said Lampe. But they never did. Werner had apparently vanished from the face of the earth.

Willi had made a big mistake. He had only meant to get Werner out of harm's way. But he had seriously underestimated Werner's resourcefulness and his resolve. And now, thanks to that misjudgment, Werner was a wanted man.

Willi went to Schobert and proposed that he should take on the case of the assault of Doctor von Fischer. After all, he knew both the victim and the perpetrator and was sure he could sort it out.

'Sort it out, Geismeier?' said Schobert. 'Are you crazy?' He jumped out of his chair. '*You?* The whole goddamned mess is your fault. Get the hell out of my office. And don't you even think of going to Captain Reineke. I know what you're thinking, Geismeier.

'You're not going anywhere near that doctor either,' said Schobert, although he half-wished Willi would, at least to avenge

Werner. But it was clear to Schobert, as it was to everyone, that Ottmar was protected on all sides, up and down the line. Getting to him now was all but impossible.

Moreover, everyone at the top, especially Police Chief Erich Lampe, understood that a thorough investigation of the attack on Ottmar would inevitably lead to a wider understanding, not only of the assault, but also inevitably of the grotesque experiments Ottmar had been conducting.

The German people were not yet ready for that, although, Lampe thought, in a few short years, once the National Socialists took power, they might be. No, no, they *would* be. But for now, Ottmar's theories and experiments had to be kept under wraps. Until their truth and usefulness could be fully understood and appreciated.

Chief Lampe was convinced Ottmar was just ahead of his time. As shocking as his work seemed at the moment, it would eventually be recognized as noble and good. Surely Ottmar von Fischer would be celebrated one day in the pantheon of German heroes working in defense of and for the advancement of the German race.

There had been a bombing at a newspaper, and there were still the missing weapons. Willi was ordered to concentrate on those cases, and amazingly he did as he was told. He continued to watch for a chance to get close to Ottmar, but the times were against him, and Ottmar vanished behind a wall of sponsors, sympathizers, and protectors.

It took a full five years for Ottmar to recover from Werner's attack. He was gradually allowed to return to his laboratory; he was reinstated as a full faculty member in the Ludwig Maximilian University School of Medicine. Professor Doctor Wilhelm August Schäuble was gone and a new hospital director, one more amenable to the rising National Socialist mood, had taken over.

Secrets get out, and in the right circles, there were whispers about Ottmar's prison experiments. They were seen in certain quarters as ahead of their time perhaps, but heroic and brave. Ottmar began to attract young disciples from among medical students and young doctors interested in the same sort of bold experimentation. One was a young Josef Mengele.

Unlike Ottmar, Mengele had no hesitation about mixing politics and science. He joined the Nazi Party, then, when the opportunity presented itself, became the chief medical officer at Auschwitz, where he applied the theories and methods pioneered by Ottmar Freiherr von Fischer on a truly horrifying scale.

Ottmar learned from his pupil too. It turned out politics and science could mix. He found his way into the SS Medical Branch where he too was finally able to do the experiments he had always dreamed of.

Between the bombing case and the stolen arms case, Willi was working long days. He saw Izabella on weekends. They were lovers, but they were not in love.

Willi came home from work late one Friday and there was a car idling in front of his house. Pinky got out carrying a package wrapped in brown paper, tied up with string.

The two men shook hands. 'This came for you,' said Pinky.

'What is it?' said Willi. Working on a bombing naturally made you nervous about packages.

Pinky seemed to read his mind. He smiled. 'It is not a bomb.' Willi's name and address were written on it in Werner Heisse's unmistakable hand. Willi took the package. At the door he turned around to look, but the car was already gone.

Inside, on top of a stack of files, was a short letter from Werner.

Greetings, Willi
I'm far away and recovering thanks to you. Me and Ilse and the cat are OK.
Here are the files from that shithead's lab. If he's still alive they should put him in Stadelheim. There's a lot of guys there would like to see him.
Be good. I know you will be. Haha
Werner